★ American Girl®

Blaire

BY JENNIFER CASTLE

Scholastic Inc.

Published by Scholastic Inc., *Publishers since 1920.* SCHOLASTIC and associated logos are trademarks and/or registered trademarks of Scholastic Inc.

The publisher does not have any control over and does not assume any responsibility for author or third-party websites or their content.

This book is a work of fiction. Names, characters, places, and incidents are either the product of the author's imagination or are used fictitiously, and any resemblance to actual persons, living or dead, business establishments, events, or locales is entirely coincidental and not intended by American Girl or Scholastic Inc.

Book design by Suzanne LaGasa

americangirl.com/service

ISBN 978-1-338-26711-2

10 9 8 7 6 5 4 3 2 1   19 20 21 22 23

Printed in the U.S.A.   23 • First printing 2019

FOR SADIE AND CLEA,
WHO MAKE EVERY DAY DELICIOUS

–J.C.

Contents

CHAPTER 1
Checking In

Some kids can't wait for the lazy, quiet days of summer.

Lazy? Quiet? No way, not at my house . . . and that's just how I like it.

Pans and dishes clang in the big kitchen. Voices chatter and silverware clinks in the dining room. Upstairs, the vacuum cleaner hums. Outside, a tractor sputters its way across a field.

Then there's the sound of the bell at the front desk, ringing one clear, musical note. *Ding.*

I turned away from the bulletin board, where I'd been pinning up a flyer for the big Ulster County Fair in August, and smiled at the man standing at the desk.

"Welcome to Pleasant View Farm Bed-and-Breakfast," I said. "Can I help you?"

"Um . . ." He hesitated, looking around for a grown-up. He was obviously surprised to be greeted by a ten-year-old girl.

I get that a lot.

"I'm Mark Reilly and I have a reservation for tonight. I know I can't check in until later, but I'm hoping I can leave a bag here while I go for a hike."

"No problem," I replied. "We can even bring it upstairs when your room is ready."

"That sounds perfect." He bent down and picked something up, then placed it delicately on the desk in front of me. "There you go."

I looked at the bag.

And the bag looked right back at me.

Or I should say, two round eyes looked back at me, through a mesh panel on the side of the bag. Whatever was in there had two huge ears and a gray nose with whiskers.

"My chinchilla, Honeybun," explained Mr. Reilly. "He's quite the traveler."

Okeydokey, I thought. I wasn't planning on babysitting a chinchilla today, but when your family's farm includes a bed-and-breakfast (especially one that advertises itself as "pet-friendly"), you pretty much expect the unexpected.

I watched Honeybun's little nose twitch. "Your buddy seems a bit nervous," I said to Mr. Reilly. "I'll bet he needs a moment to relax."

"He would like that," Mr. Reilly said, his face softening with relief. "Somewhere dark and quiet."

I nodded. "I know just the place."

"Thank you." Then he said good-bye to us both and left.

I picked up Honeybun's carrier bag and walked past the restaurant dining room and the door to the restaurant kitchen, then down a hallway. At the back of our house was a second, smaller kitchen—the one our family used—and my grandfather's bedroom.

"You'll be comfy in here for a while," I said to Honeybun as I put him on Grandpa's desk in the corner. "I'll come back for you a little later."

I turned to leave the room, only to be stopped short as my dress caught on the bag's zipper and pulled it open.

Uh-oh.

Before I knew it, there was a flash of gray fur and a puffy tail moving past me. I squealed as the gray blob raced around my grandfather's room, almost faster than I could keep track of him. Under the bed! Under the desk! Under the chair! And then . . .

Stillness. Where had he gone?! I could already picture Mr. Reilly's review on the travel sites: *ZERO stars!!! Pleasant View Farm Bed-and-Breakfast LOST my chinchilla!!!!!*

Don't panic, I told myself. *This is your house, not Honeybun's, and you know every nook and cranny.*

I got down on my hands and knees, peeking under Grandpa's bed. I saw something fuzzy. "Honeybun! Thank goodness," I said, reaching for the chinchilla. "It's okay, little guy. Let's get you back in your bag where you'll be safe." I pulled him out slowly and started petting . . . Grandpa's old slipper. Great. I'd been talking to a shoe.

Still on my hands and knees, I checked under the dresser. Nothing. I looked behind Grandpa's hamper. No chinchilla, just one dirty sock that hadn't made it into the basket. *Eww.*

As I crawled slowly toward the door, I scanned the room, checking the corners. I poked my head into the hallway, calling a soft, "Here, chilla, chilla, chilla," hoping Honeybun would come running like a cat.

Nope. Instead I saw Grandpa standing at the other end of the hall, looking at me with a confused expression. He was with a young couple, and the woman was holding a squirming toddler by the hand.

"Blaire?" asked Grandpa, peering at me over the top of his glasses. "What on earth are you doing down there?"

I jumped up and brushed myself off. "I . . . was . . . uh . . . trying to see which floorboard is the one that always creaks when you step on it," I stammered, walking back to the front desk. "Doesn't that bug you? It really bugs me!"

Grandpa raised an eyebrow. "It's been one of the biggest mysteries of my life." He knew something was up. "In the meantime," he continued, "Blaire, these are the Springers. They came here on their honeymoon a few years ago, and now they're back with their son, Aiden."

"Oh, I remember you guys!" I said, turning in a slow circle and looking for any signs of Honeybun. The little boy let go of his mom's hand and started spinning in a circle, too. I caught his eye and he giggled.

"We remember you, too," Mr. Springer said. "We've been following the cooking posts you do with your mom on the farm's website."

I stopped spinning. "Thanks!" Mom and I have fun posting recipes and cooking videos. It's always cool to be reminded that people actually read them.

"And it looks like you all have a big project going on with your old barn," added Mrs. Springer. "I saw your father working out there."

"Yep," I replied, peeking behind the long curtains that covered the front windows. "We're converting it into an event space for parties and weddings."

At the word *weddings*, Grandpa cleared his throat. He wasn't too supportive of our family's new business venture. "I hope you'll enjoy your stay," Grandpa said, changing the subject.

"Thank you," said Mrs. Springer, hurrying after Aiden, who had stopped spinning and was now headed for the front door. "Something tells me it won't be quite as restful this time."

I was just about to look for Honeybun behind the pillows on the window seat when Aiden started crying. His mom had picked him up, and he was not happy. Okay, the chinchilla would have to wait. I cannot let little kids cry at Pleasant View Farm.

"Aiden," I said brightly. "Come with me."

Mrs. Springer and Aiden followed me to the wall under the big staircase. Hidden in the patterned wallpaper was a tiny doorknob, easy to miss if you didn't know to look for it. I opened a little door, and as soon as he saw what was inside, Aiden stopped crying and squirmed out of his mom's arms.

I'd spent months turning a storage space under the stairs into a play kitchen for kids and families who visited the B and B and the restaurant. It was an idea I'd gotten from one of my favorite design bloggers about doing creative things with unused spaces. Dad and I had a blast building a miniature pretend stove and fridge, and I'd filled it with toy pots, pans, dishes, and food. We even made a kid-sized table and two chairs, and I painted windows with curtains on the walls.

Mrs. Springer and I crawled in after Aiden. "Oh, Blaire," she said, "this is absolutely delightf*aaaahhhh!*"

A puffy gray blob darted into the room and did a figure eight around Mrs. Springer's ankles.

"What was that?" she shrieked as Grandpa and Mr. Springer came running.

"Honeybun!" I shouted.

"Honey who?" Grandpa shouted back.

I didn't stop to answer. Honeybun scrambled out of the play kitchen, dashed across the hall, and raced toward the dining room. I ran after him and—*BAM*.

I collided with my seven-year-old brother, Beckett.

"I just saw a giant mouse!" he exclaimed.

"It's a chinchilla, and he's one of our guests," I replied. "Help me catch him!"

We ran into the dining room. Luckily it was empty. I remembered what Mr. Reilly had said about keeping Honeybun calm, so I closed the door, turned off the lights, and told Beckett to stay quiet.

"Where is he?" Beckett whispered after a few moments.

"There!" I whispered, pointing to a tail sticking out from underneath a tablecloth.

Beckett dove under the table . . . and Honeybun scurried out the other side.

"Over there!" I whispered, as Honeybun disappeared under a different table. Beckett followed him, but the same thing happened.

"Table by the fireplace!" I whispered. This time I crouched on one side of the table while Beckett guarded the other. For a few moments, nothing—and no one—moved. I plucked a cloth napkin off the table as the corner of the table cloth twitched. *One . . . two . . . three . . .*

"Gotcha!" I grabbed Honeybun and wrapped him in the napkin. Rodent rescued!

Back in Grandpa's room, I put Honeybun in his carrier while Beckett zipped up the opening as fast as he could. "That's enough excitement for you, Honeybun," I said. "You deserve a nap."

I high-fived Beckett. "Thanks for your help."

"That was fun," Beckett said. He was always catching something in the creek on our farm, so this was probably not the only critter he'd be chasing today.

For me, one was enough.

When I went back out front, the Springers were gone. "I'm sure there's a reasonable explanation for all of that," said Grandpa from behind the desk.

"Of course," I replied. But before I could say any more, my mother popped her head out the door of the restaurant kitchen, where she was the chef.

"Blaire, can you go pick more sugar snap peas? I have some time to work on our recipe for the website before lunch service starts."

"You got it," I replied.

"Thanks. Hey, what was all that racket in the dining room?" she asked.

"Oh, you know," I said, "just another day at Pleasant View Farm."

CHAPTER 2

Super Scrumptious

Mom was washing strawberries and blueberries when I entered the restaurant kitchen with the basketful of sugar snap peas. A bowl of fresh greens and a camera sat on the counter nearby. Beckett and I had picked the berries and greens that morning. Mom's restaurant is "farm to table," which means we grow many of the ingredients right here on our farm. What we can't grow ourselves, we get from other farms in the area. Mom cooks with what's in season so that everything is super fresh and totally delicious.

"Here you go," I said, setting the basket on the counter. "Sssss-super sssss-scrumptious ssssss-snap peas for the sssssss-summer sssss-salad!"

All those *s*'s were our little joke for the most popular item on our summer menu. "And warm from the ssss-sunshine, too. Thanks, ssss-sweetie," Mom replied.

We giggled as we got to work on the salad. I love hanging out in this kitchen with Mom before the restaurant opens and the room gets busy with kitchen staff. As she sautéed the sugar snap peas, I took photos of her for the website, and Mom took photos of me when I mixed the blueberry vinaigrette dressing. The dressing was a recipe I invented last summer when we had a bumper crop of our blueberries, and customers loved it. Now it was on the menu as "Blaire-berry Vinaigrette."

When the peas were done, I placed them on the plate, along with the greens, and arranged the strawberries in a ring on top. The different shades of the veggies mixed just right with the reds of the berries. Now I just had to add the dressing . . . *Perfect.*

As Mom balanced on a step stool to get some shots of the finished dish from above, I started cleaning up the kitchen. There was a smushed blueberry on the counter, and I grabbed a paper towel to wipe it up. I was about to throw the paper towel away when I noticed the color on it. Not blue exactly, but not quite purple either. Ideasparks started going off in my head. I knew I could make something crafty with that color—maybe a decoration for the front desk. I folded the paper towel into a tiny square and tucked it into my pocket.

"Think about what you want to say about this recipe, and we can post it tonight," Mom said, putting the rest of the salad ingredients into the giant refrigerator. She glanced at the clock. "Don't you need to get ready for Thea's party?"

"Oh my gosh, you're right. I still have to wrap her present."

"Then go, go, go—and have fun!"

"Thanks, Mom." I kissed her good-bye and dashed out the door.

Our house, a Victorian built over a hundred years ago, has a narrow back staircase running up from the family kitchen. I took the steps two at a time past the second floor, where our guests stayed, to the third floor, where my parents, brother, and I lived.

I bounded down the hallway to the best room in the whole house: my turret bedroom. It had been Mom's room when she was growing up. When I opened the door, the sunlight practically blinded me, but hey, small price to pay when one whole wall of your room is a semicircle of ginormous windows.

I took the paper towel out of my pocket and headed over to my inspiration board, which was where my random idea-sparks ended up. I pinned the blueberry smear to one corner, in between a magazine clipping of party decorations and a sunny yellow fabric swatch.

After I changed into my swimsuit, shorts, and a T-shirt, I sat down at my desk to wrap the gift for my BFF's birthday. I'd spent a week making her a pillow based on one we'd seen online. I'd never done anything quite like it before, and it was super fun to make it up as I went along. I was really happy with the way it turned out—one whole side was sequins!—and I couldn't wait to see Thea's face when she opened it. But now it was time for the finishing touch—a homemade gift tag. I took the strip of photos of me and Thea off my inspiration board. They were from the photo booth at last year's fair.

After cutting one photo off and punching a hole in the corner, I attached it to the package with a ribbon and wrote a note on the back.

Done!

I pinned the rest of the photo booth strip back on the inspiration board (my BFF was always a huge inspiration to me), then headed downstairs with the gift. There was a mix of voices in the dining room, which meant that lunch service had already started. I poked my head around the corner and saw one of the waitstaff putting a plate of summer salad down in front of a customer.

The customer lifted her fork.

I held my breath and thought of planting the snap peas and pruning the strawberry runners. I thought of the hours Mom and I spent in the kitchen, experimenting and sampling recipes. It was all for this. To give someone a *delicious* moment.

"Oh my WOW," the customer said. She put her fork down and looked at her friend across the table. "I think this is the best salad I've ever tasted."

"I told you, that dressing is insane," said the friend.

A familiar warm, winning feeling rushed through me as I headed out the front door. *Yes! I never get tired of that.*

I walked across our circular driveway and down a dirt path to a big old red barn. The tap-tap-tap of a hammer got louder as I got closer.

"Dad?" I called once I was inside. My father was up in the loft, fitting the joints of two wooden beams together. He looked down at me, two nails sticking out of his mouth.

"Hey, kiddo," he said, but with the nails in his mouth it sounded more like, "Hakkkkkiddddo."

"Time to go," I said. "Thea's party, remember?"

"How could I forget the official start of summer?" Dad said.

As he climbed down the ladder, I took a look around the barn. He was making steady progress, working in the barn whenever he had time left over from running the business and marketing sides of Pleasant View Farm. With the new ceiling beams in place now, idea-sparks started going off in my head again. Shimmery silver streamers hanging from one beam as a backdrop for a photo booth. Light-up, gigantic paper stars strung from the others. I had a zillion ideas . . . but they would have to wait. The barn wouldn't be ready for months.

"Dad! Come on!" I said.

A few minutes later, we were in his truck on the road into town, the Shawangunk Ridge mountains disappearing behind us. As the woods on the side of the road rushed by, I rolled down the window and took a big breath in. The air smelled sweet and fresh and full of possibility.

CHAPTER 3

My New Normal

We'd barely pulled into the parking lot of Hudson Point Park when I spotted my best friend, Theodora Dimitriou. Well, it was hard to miss her. She was standing next to the park pavilion, wearing a green bathing suit, a fluffy yellow feather boa, big black sunglasses, and a plastic tiara that read BIRTHDAY GIRL in glittering pink letters.

As soon as Dad stopped the car, I grabbed my towel and Thea's gift and hopped out.

"*Dahhling!*" Thea said in the fake English accent she sometimes likes to do. "Thank goodness you're here."

"I wouldn't miss it for the *world*," I answered in my fake English accent, which wasn't nearly as good as Thea's. "Happy birthday!" I gave her a giant hug. The feather boa tickled my nose!

"Thanks!" said Thea in her regular voice. "Happy summer. Two months of swimming and slumber parties and movies and—"

"—the county fair," we said together.

"We are going to have so much fun," I said, waving good-bye to Dad.

Thea grabbed my hand and dragged me toward the pebbly beach. Hudson Point Park is on an inlet of the Hudson River, where you can swim and go kayaking. Our other friends were already in the water: Rosie and Sabrina were practicing handstands, and Piper, Amadi, and Victoria seemed to be having a splash war, though I wasn't sure who was winning.

"Speaking of fun," I said to Thea as I kicked off my sandals and peeled off my clothes, "you'll never guess what I did this morning." We joined our friends in the river, and I told everyone about Honeybun's escape. Thea did a hilarious impersonation of a chinchilla on the run. By the time Mrs. Dimitriou called us up to the pavilion to eat, everyone's stomach hurt from laughing.

"I'm starving," Piper said as we walked across the sand.

My own stomach growled, but when we reached the food table, I stopped short. My good mood disappeared faster than a chinchilla racing through a B and B.

Pizza: Can't have that.

Cheese and crackers: Only if I skip the cheese.

Sour cream dip: Nope, no way.

There was other food to choose from, but all I could see was the dairy stuff I couldn't have.

It had only been two weeks since I'd sat in an office with Mom and Dad, listening to a doctor talk about my test results. "Blaire has lactose intolerance," she'd told us.

"Lactose intolerance" explained why I've had a lot of bloating, bellyaches, and other tummy trouble this year. It had all gotten so bad that Mom took me to see a pediatric gastroenterologist, a doctor who treats kids with digestive problems. He told us there was good news. I didn't need medicine, surgery, or anything like that. "Treatment is easy-peasy," he'd said.

Easy-peasy for him to say. He wasn't the one who had to stop eating all dairy foods overnight. Hopefully, I'll be able to eat dairy again. Someday. Until we knew how serious my intolerance was, we had to be super strict about it. Absolutely no dairy for the next three months.

"It'll be an adjustment," he'd said as he handed my mom a packet of information on how to eat dairy-free. "Try to think of this as your 'new normal.'"

Well, so far, my new normal was the worst. As Sabrina grabbed a piece of gooey cheese pizza, my eyes stung with tears.

I took some veggies, fruit, crackers, and chips and squeezed into a spot at the table between Amadi and Rosie. Thankfully, no one seemed to notice that I skipped half the food.

But a little while later, when Thea's dad brought out the birthday cake, Mrs. Dimitriou placed a single cupcake in front of me.

"It's dairy-free," Thea announced. "The man at the bakery said you can't even tell the difference."

I gave Thea a surprised look. She was the only friend I'd told about my new normal, and I'd asked her to keep it a secret.

"Wait a sec," Piper said. "Blaire can't eat dairy? Since when?"

Now everyone was staring at me. They were all my friends, but I didn't want to talk about this. Not at Thea's party. I shrugged. "A couple of weeks ago."

"Can you eat *any* dairy?" Victoria asked. "Cheese? Butter? Milk?"

I shook my head.

"What about soy milk?" asked Sabrina.

"What about ice cream?" Piper added, sounding really worried.

I didn't say anything. Out on the river, one of the boats sounded its horn. I considered swimming out there, getting on the boat, and sailing away from this conversation.

Mr. Dimitriou lit the candles on the cake. "Let's sing!" he said.

I did my best to belt out "Happy Birthday" along with everyone else, but I couldn't help feeling a little irritated at Thea for spilling the beans about my food issue.

While Mr. Dimitriou passed out pieces of cake, Sabrina pointed to my cupcake, which had white frosting and silver sprinkles.

"It's so pretty!" she said. "How does it taste?"

I took a tiny bite. It wasn't the cream cheese frosting I loved. And it felt super weird to be eating something different from everyone else. "Yummy," I said, trying to sound enthusiastic. I didn't want Thea to feel bad.

Thea put her arm around me and gave me a squeeze.

"I'm sorry you had to buy special food for me," I muttered. "It's so embarrassing."

"Don't feel embarrassed," she said.

"Tons of people have food allergies," added Rosie. "My cousin can't eat anything with peanuts in it."

"Can't you take medicine?" Sabrina asked. "My brother's lactose intolerant, and he just takes a pill before he eats dairy stuff."

"Tried that," I said softly. "Didn't work for me. Sometimes that happens, I guess."

Amadi said, "Hey, wait. Are you going to be able to cook?" She put down her fork.

That was one big question I'd been asking myself. If I couldn't eat some of the ingredients in my favorite recipes anymore, could I still make those foods? How could I cook something like crème brûlée—one of my specialties!—and then *not* eat it?

Mrs. Dimitriou touched my hand. "Blaire will find a way to do what she loves. She's a born chef. That's who she is."

No, I thought. *That's who I WAS.*

"Time for gifts!" Thea's dad said a few minutes later. Everyone gathered around Thea, who was smiling about as big as I'd ever seen her smile. We'd been BFFs since we were five, and we'd always been together on our birthdays. But the truth was, right now I just didn't want to be here. I turned to Thea's mom.

"Mrs. Dimitriou?" I said quietly. "I'm not feeling so well. Can you call someone at the farm to come pick me up?"

She searched my face for a moment before she said, "Of course, sweetie. I'm sorry to hear that." She made the call, then told me Grandpa was on his way.

I was super relieved to see his van show up a few minutes later. Thea stopped her gift-opening to walk me to the parking lot.

"We're going out on the kayaks after gifts. Are you sure you won't stay?"

"Yeah . . ." I said. "I'm sorry."

"No—I'm sorry about the cupcake. I just wanted you to have something special while we had cake."

"I know you meant well," I said. "I'm just not ready to talk about it with everyone yet."

I gave my BFF a quick, awkward hug, then climbed into the van, trying not to cry.

CHAPTER 4

Cute Little Stinkers

I stared at the app on Grandpa's phone. **THIS OR THAT? BEING ABLE TO FLY or TELEKINESIS.**

This game was one of my favorites, and right now it was way more fun than thinking about what a disaster that party had been.

Telekinesis, hands down. I touched that choice on the screen.

"Your mom said you weren't feeling well, sweetheart," Grandpa said. "Did you eat something that made you sick?"

"Nope," I said, swiping to the next question.

THIS OR THAT? DOG FOOD FOR DINNER or FISH FOOD IN YOUR WATER BOTTLE. *Um, neither?* But I picked fish food since that was probably dairy-free.

Grandpa kept talking. "Then why did you leave the party early? You're always the last to leave that group of giggly girls."

I shrugged without looking up from his phone.

"And it's not like you to have your nose buried in a screen," Grandpa said.

I didn't answer. Suddenly, he made a sharp right turn. That made me look up. "Hey," I said. "This isn't how we go home."

"I was on my way somewhere when your mom called me to come get you. We're headed there now." He glanced at me and the phone in my hand. "I might even tell you where, if you put that thing down so we can have a real conversation."

I sighed and placed his phone on the seat next to me.

"Do you remember my friend Freddy and his farm, Moonlight Meadow?" asked Grandpa.

"Oh yeah," I said. "He breeds animals, right?"

Grandpa nodded. "Goats and sheep." Then his voice got quieter. "He's shutting down and selling off the land. He's getting rid of some furniture, and I'm going to take a look at it, for the B and B."

"That's so sad," I said. "Why's he closing the farm?"

"Too much competition in the livestock business," replied Grandpa. "It's a common story these days. Small farms—no matter what they raise or grow—have to work harder and harder to stay afloat."

"But Pleasant View Farm is okay, right?" I asked. As far as I could tell, our farm wasn't in danger.

"Actually, business is good," Grandpa said. "The crops, the restaurant, the inn are all going well, but they're a lot to keep track of. So why take on more—like fixing up that barn?"

I perked up at the mention of the barn. I knew Grandpa wasn't crazy about the project, but I couldn't wait for it to be finished. "I think the barn's going to be awesome," I said, smiling for the first time since leaving the lake. "The parties and weddings are going to make people happy, and we get to be part of it all."

Grandpa shook his head. "I'm too old to be part of it all anymore."

"Grandpa!" I scolded. "You're not *that* old. Just wait. I'll show you how much fun it will be."

"Hmph," Grandpa answered, pulling into Freddy's long dirt driveway.

When we got to the house, Grandpa and Freddy went into the living room and I used the bathroom to change out of my damp bathing suit. When I came back out a few minutes later, I overheard Grandpa and Freddy laughing.

"Weddings?" Freddy asked. "That's craziness. You folks have your hands full as it is. More than full."

"Exactly," said Grandpa. "Why risk ruining everything we've spent so many years building? But I can't talk them out of it."

I crept a little closer so I could hear better.

"I think it might be time for me to retire," Grandpa continued. "I can't take the headache. You and I could pack up and move to Florida.

WHAT??? Freddy was saying something, but I didn't want to hear any more. I hurried out of the house and down a dirt path to Freddy's livestock barn. My head was spinning.

Grandpa would *retire*? He was the heart and history of Pleasant View Farm. What would we do without him?

I reached the barn and stepped inside. The space had an empty quiet, and it made me sad to know that all the animals were gone.

Baaaaah.

Or maybe not.

The sound had come from the other end of the building. I walked down the aisle, past one empty pen after another.

Baaaaah.

Now I saw two little ears, low to the ground.

I peered over the gate of one pen . . . and OH. MY. GOSH.

A lamb. Snuggled up on some hay. And . . .

OH MY DOUBLE GOSH.

There was a tiny brown goat, too, curled up next to the lamb. It had a black stripe down its back and black legs that made it look like it was wearing boots.

"Hi, babies!!!" I squealed, leaning over the gate and stretching out my hand. The lamb sniffed my fingers, its wide, dark eyes staring up at me, like it had been waiting for me to get here.

Baaaaah.

Now the goat opened its eyes. *Maaaaah.*

"Awwwww," I replied.

There was laughter behind me, and I turned to see Freddy and Grandpa.

"They're cute little stinkers, aren't they?" said Freddy. He sighed. "The lamb wouldn't nurse, and the goat was sick, so I ended up bottle-feeding them both and keeping them in the same pen. Now they can't be separated and I'll have to find a place that will take them together."

"They need a home?" I asked.

Freddy nodded.

I looked at Grandpa with my best puppy-dog eyes. No—my best little *lamb* eyes.

"Blaire . . ." Grandpa said, shaking his head. "We were *just* talking about how there's no reason for our farm to take on anything new right now."

"But this isn't anything new!" I burst out. "There's that old shed and a pen right next to the chicken coop. You said you used to have animals there. So really, it's an old thing."

Grandpa's face softened. "That's true. I helped my dad build that shed when I was no older than you are now." He came closer to look into the stall. "We had goats and lambs, too—sold the milk and the wool. Folks loved visiting with the animals when they stopped by our farm stand."

"I read that goats eat poison ivy and stuff," I said. "So it would *help* the farm. And guests at the inn and the bistro would love a petting zoo. Especially families."

"A farm with farm animals," said Freddy. "There's no craziness in that, Ben. I'll throw in the feed and milk replacer I have left, too. They'll need formula once a day for a few more weeks."

"You both drive a hard bargain," Grandpa said. He looked at me. "Blaire, this is the happiest you've looked since I picked you up. We'll take 'em! I have no idea what your mom and dad will say, but leave that part to me."

I threw my arms around his neck and kissed his cheek. "Thank you!"

Before I knew it, I was riding in the back of the van next to a giant animal crate. Inside, Penelope the lamb (named after my favorite DIY craft video blogger) and Dash the goat (because he had that super cool black racing stripe) were snuggled up together. I thought about how the day had started with a chinchilla on the loose in the house and ended up with two new baby animals for the farm. (I was just going to ignore the cupcake catastrophe in the middle.)

Things had gone from bad to good in a way I never expected. Maybe there was a way I could turn Grandpa's opinion of the barn from bad to good, too. All I needed was a real event to show him the possibilities.

CHAPTER 5

Best Idea Ever

S top! Aagh! That tickles!"
I'd barely stepped into the pen when Penelope and
Dash came at me, tails wagging and heads nudging the
bottles in my hands. I didn't think I could feed them both
at once, so I stuck Dash's bottle behind me, in the waist of
my shorts. I squeezed a few drops of lamb milk replacer
from Penny's bottle onto my palm to make sure it wasn't
too hot, like Freddy had shown me the day before.
Penelope was not exactly patient. She kept jumping up
and putting her front hooves on my stomach.

"Okay, okay, *okay*," I said, giving Penny her bottle.
She started suckling at it so hard that she almost pulled
it out of my hand. Her ears wiggled as she drank, which
was crazy adorable. It seemed pretty easy until I felt
something yank at the back of my pants.

I looked behind me to see Dash grabbing at the bottle
in my waistband. I spun around so Dash couldn't get it,

but since Penny refused to let go of *her* bottle, she spun around with me and crashed into Dash. Then Dash's bottle fell out of my waistband, onto the ground. I reached for it. So did Dash. I got to it before he did, but Penny's suckling knocked me off-balance. The next thing I knew, I was lying in the dirt, covered in hay, holding two bottles for the animals hovering above me.

"Is that the way you're supposed to do it?" asked Beckett, who was suddenly standing in the pen, holding a fitness ball.

"Probably not," I said. "Would you help me?"

"Can I?" Beckett dropped the fitness ball, plopped down in the hay, and took Dash's bottle. He giggled as the goat stayed glued to the bottle. Beckett had been thrilled yesterday when Grandpa and I introduced him to the animals. Mom and Dad were a little less enthused, but they came around.

"What's the ball for?" I asked Beckett as Dash finished his bottle.

"Grandpa said I should try this." Beckett rolled the ball across the pen and Dash chased it down, then tried to jump on top of it. He balanced there for two seconds, then tumbled off. Beckett cracked up. He rolled the ball again, and Dash did the same balancing trick.

"That's so cute," I said. "Maybe you can teach him to do other tricks. You two could perform at the county fair in August."

"Great idea!" Beckett said. As I headed over to the chicken coop, Beckett was saying, "Come on, Dash. Let's try again." I had to laugh. I wasn't serious, but if Beckett wanted to try to train a goat, he should go for it.

"Hello, ladies," I said as I opened the gate to the chicken coop. "I'm guessing you've noticed your new neighbors by now?"

The chickens answered me in their low-pitched, repeating *cluck cluck cluck* known as a "contentment call." It meant they were happy to see me, and the feeling was totally mutual.

I scattered chicken feed and watched the birds peck at the dirt. Then I picked up my favorite, a super soft white Silkie chicken I'd named Dandelion, because her fluffy head looked like the dandelion puffs that grew along the fence by the vegetable fields. She started clucking.

"What's that?" I held her up to my ear and turned my head so I could listen to what she was saying. Over in the pen, Beckett was still playing ball with Dash. "Yeah, Beckett's pretty happy about the new animals. You know who else is?"

Dandy cocked her head, giving me her full attention. She's a great listener.

"That's right," I answered, walking to the other side of the coop. "Grandpa. He's really glad the animals are here. Maybe they'll take his mind off the barn. But if they don't," I continued, "then *whatever* that first barn event is, *whenever* it is, I'm going to make sure it's the Best Barn Event Ever, so Grandpa won't possibly want to leave. Think I can do it, Dandy?"

She moved her head up and down, like she was nodding.

Chickens: the ultimate confidence boosters.

As I put Dandy down, a voice from outside the coop said, "Should I call you Old MacDonald now that you have so many farm animals?"

It was Caterina Minardi, our farm manager. She's the coolest grown-up I know.

"Did you met Penelope and Dash?" I asked, coming out of the coop and closing the gate tightly behind me.

"Beckett made the introductions," she said, giving me a hug.

Cat is twenty-eight, but she seems more like a teenager to me. She wears ripped jeans, work boots with rainbow-striped laces, and funky T-shirts. Today's tee had a picture of a princess climbing down a stone tower, with the words I WILL RESCUE MYSELF, THANKS underneath.

Cat pulled straw out of my hair as I told her about my first attempt to feed two hungry baby animals. "Chickens are definitely easier," I said. "How did things go in Kingston yesterday?" Cat takes produce from Pleasant View Farm to sell at the big farmers' market every week.

"We sold everything I brought. How was Thea's party?"

Ugh. Thea's party. I changed the subject. "Time for our Saturday morning field date!" I offered my hand up for a high five.

"You know it, Sprout," Cat said as she slapped my palm. "It's my favorite time of the week."

Sprout is her nickname for me because that's what her father called her when she was growing up on her own family's farm, and because she says it makes her happy to be reminded of another generation of farmers. Cat's parents both passed away years ago and Lorenzo, her only sibling, is in the Marines and lives two thousand miles away on a military base in Arizona.

We're like a substitute family for Cat, and I'll take her as my big sister any day.

We headed to the vegetable fields, where we grow food in bigger quantities than the kitchen gardens. I waved at some of the farm crew working another field.

"Squash seeds," Cat said when we got to a patch of tilled soil. She showed me how deep to plant the seeds. As we worked, I thought of how the tiny seeds would grow into bright gold butternut squash. I pictured myself working with Mom in the kitchen, peeling the squash, chopping it, and roasting it with olive oil and cinnamon. *YUM.*

We worked for a while, until we heard the sound of bike tires on the gravel path bordering the field.

"Looks like my lunch has arrived," said Cat with a smile. Her boyfriend, Gabe, popped a wheelie before sliding to a stop beside us.

"Show-off," Cat teased, then gave him a quick kiss hello.

"Can't help it," Gabe said. "Gotta impress my two favorite girls." He hopped off the bike and pulled a brown paper sack out of one of his saddlebags. I recognized the logo on it: It was from the deli next to the bike shop where Gabe worked.

"Turkey sub on wheat for Cat." Out of the other saddlebag, he pulled two packages of snacks. "I got these for you, Blaire. Take your pick!"

I looked at the choices: potato chips and white cheddar popcorn. It was sweet of him to bring me something, but . . . seriously? I'm not even safe from dairy out here in a *vegetable field*?

"Thanks," I said. "I'll take the chips."

If Cat is my pretend big sister, Gabe is like a big brother, and he's always super thoughtful. In the two years he and Cat have been dating, he's brought picnic lunches to her once a week—even in the winter. Cat says he's the best boyfriend ever.

"I'll go wash my hands," Cat said, heading toward the greenhouse on the other side of the field. "Meet you at the gazebo?"

"See you there," Gabe said.

I couldn't help but smile. The gazebo is their special picnic spot. Dad had built the gazebo right on the edge of the creek, with two bench seats inside.

"Have a good lunch," I said to Gabe, "and thanks again for the—"

"Blaire!" Gabe interrupted me in a shaky whisper. "I need your help."

My help? "What's the matter?" I asked.

"Just . . ." Gabe glanced toward Cat, who was still walking toward the greenhouse. "Just . . . come on, I'll tell you on the way."

"Okaaaayyy," I said, "but you're kind of freaking me out."

We walked in silence down the dirt path and under the archway at the entrance to the orchard. Once we reached the trees, Gabe stopped and turned to me.

"So the thing is," he began. He paused dramatically . . . then his serious expression opened into a huge grin. "I want to ask Cat to marry me."

"What? Oh, Gabe. She'll be so happy!" I jumped up and down. More straw fell out of my hair.

"I hope you're right," he said. "We've never even talked about marriage, so honestly, I'm not sure what she'll think. You know how Cat likes her independence."

"But she loves you," I reminded him. "How could she say no? That would be so mean!"

"Well, Cat always says what she feels, and I love that about her. If she's not ready to get married, she'll turn me down. But *I'm* ready, so I have to ask."

"Oh, I hope-hope-hope she says yes!!!" I gave him a big hug.

"I'm glad we have your blessing," he said when I finally let go. "But here's the thing. Cat's one of a kind, so I want her proposal to be one of a kind, too. That's where you come in."

"Me?"

"Will you be my proposal assistant?" Gabe asked.

Proposal assistant? I had no idea what that was, but that didn't stop me from wanting to do it!

"I will!" I said. "What are your ideas so far?"

"I definitely want it to happen here at the farm, and there should be some surprises," Gabe said. "I need a hand making the whole thing as special as Cat is."

"You're talking to the right assistant," I said. Idea-sparks were already bursting in my brain. "We'll need decorations. And food," I said as we started walking toward the creek. "Wait—I might need some help. Can I tell my mom? And Thea?"

"Okay, but don't let Cat find out."

"You got it," I said, flashing him a thumbs-up. Then I skipped back through the rows of apple trees toward the house.

※

"Hey, Mom," I said as I rushed through the kitchen door. "I have news. You're going to flip."

"In a good way, I hope," she said. She was standing at the stove, stirring something in a big pot.

"Gabe's planning to propose to Cat," I whispered. "And he asked me to help him!"

Plop. Mom had clapped her hands together, which made her drop the spoon into the pot. "That's wonderful news!"

"Do you think Cat will say yes?" I asked, leaning against the counter.

"Well, marriage is a big deal," Mom said. "She may want to think it over. But Gabe seems like a terrific guy, and they look so happy together."

"If I make this proposal super awesome, she won't have any choice but to say yes!"

Mom laughed. "That sounds like a Blaire strategy! Just let me know if you need a hand. You'll make crème brûlée, right? It's Cat's favorite."

My crème brûlée *is* Cat's favorite. But I haven't cooked anything with dairy in it since being diagnosed as lactose intolerant. I'm not sure I could do it, even for

Cat. "You may need to make this batch," I told Mom. "I'll be pretty busy with decorations." Then I changed the subject. "What's that?" I gestured to the pot on the stove. "Red pepper sauce?"

"Yep. I'm experimenting with something new for the menu. Don't you think this would be terrific on zucchini noodles? Wait . . . what did I do with my spoon?"

I pointed to the pot and tried not to laugh.

"Oh my goodness!" she said, fishing out the spoon and wiping the handle. "What would I do without my official taste tester? Want to give your opinion?"

Mom scooped up some of the sauce with the spoon and held it out. The sauce looked as delicious as it smelled, rich and creamy . . .

CREAMY.

I stepped back.

"Mom, if that has cream in it, I can't." *This is why I can't cook right now*, I thought. A chef has to taste what she's making.

"Oh, Blaire," said Mom, her face falling. "I'm so sorry. I completely forgot. I'm still getting used to this whole thing, just like you."

Beckett appeared behind Mom. He must have come in through the family kitchen.

"Hey, if Blaire can't be your taste tester anymore, can I do it?" he asked.

My mouth fell open, but no words came out. Beckett? A taste tester? The kid eats dirt! But that wasn't what made tears sting my eyes. I left the kitchen and ran up three flights of stairs to my room, wondering what kind of a cook I was now.

CHAPTER 6
Sneaky Stuff

"Goat on the go!" Thea exclaimed, laughing as Dash skidded down the slide. Grandpa had set up an old plastic play set in the animals' pen—the one Beckett and I outgrew years ago—and now it was farm baby recess all the time.

I'd texted Thea the night before to tell her my two pieces of big news. She was thrilled about Gabe's proposal, but when she heard about Penelope and Dash . . . well, let's just say that if Thea could have climbed through the computer screen to get to the farm, she totally would have. We were so busy squealing about the animals that Thea didn't say anything about me leaving her birthday party early. That was okay with me.

Dash hopped back up onto the top of the play set, where Thea was sitting, and nibbled at her ear.

"Dash!" Thea exclaimed. "That tickles."

"Dash, no!" I said, grabbing the headband from Thea's hair as Dash tried to take a bite of it. "He'll eat anything," I explained to Thea.

For the next hour, I took pictures and videos of Penny and Dash with my tablet. They were going to be a huge hit on the farm's website. But eventually, the slide wore them out and they fell asleep curled up together by the shed.

"Okay, back to the proposal," Thea said. "What did you and Gabe talk about last night?"

"We were brainstorming, and since he and Cat both like games—"

"Oh yeah!" Thea exclaimed. "Remember that night we played Monopoly with them? Gabe was so mad that I beat him. That's when he started calling me—"

"*Deadly Dimitriou.* And you were," I said, shaking my head at the memory of Thea's killer Monopoly skills. "Anyway, we've decided to do a sort of scavenger hunt, with Gabe planting a trail of notes for Cat to follow around the farm. They'll end on the restaurant patio. That's where Gabe will propose."

"I love it," said Thea. "That's so much better than how that guy proposed to his girlfriend on *Dress Quest* last week. Did you see it?"

Dress Quest is one of our favorite shows. A hidden camera captures the couple's proposal, then follows the girl as she shops for her wedding dress at the famous Kellenberger's salon in Manhattan. "Oh, totally," I said. "That proposal with the ring in the dessert was so boring! A million people have done that!"

"But wait," Thea said. She sat up and crossed her legs. "Don't you think Cat will suspect it's a proposal before she even gets to the patio? I mean, notes from Gabe all over the farm is kind of a giveaway."

"Yeah, I had the same thought. I need to figure that out."

Thea's face lit up with an idea. "What if you made it look like the clues are from you and Beckett? Like, you're the ones playing the game with her? She wouldn't even know Gabe's behind it until she gets to the end."

"Oh, Thea!" I said. "Brilliant. You're so good at this sneaky stuff."

"I knooooow," she replied in an "evil villain" voice, stroking an imaginary beard. "Being devious is my specialty."

"So when Cat walks onto the patio, she needs to know instantly that what she's seeing is from Gabe, not us. It needs to be romantic." I closed my eyes, and it came to me in an idea-spark. "What if there were dozens of paper-bag lanterns? We could use bags from the deli where Gabe gets sandwiches for their picnic lunches."

"Ooh, that's good," Thea said.

I turned to my tablet and started browsing for paper-bag-lantern photos.

"So I have some news of my own," Thea said.

"Oh yeah? What?" My tablet screen filled with images. *WHOA.* Who knew there were five bajillion different types of paper-bag lanterns? And that they're called *luminarias*? My head started spinning with all the possibilities.

"The director of my dance troupe asked me to perform with them at the county fair on August third," Thea continued.

"Really?" I looked up from the tablet. The county fair is more than a major summer event around Bluefield—it's a tradition for Thea and me. We take silly photos in the old-timey photo booth, go through the fun house as many times as we can, watch the older kids in her dance troupe perform, and most importantly, get a giant funnel cake covered in whipped cream. Oh, man. I'll have to skip the whipped cream this year. I turned back to my tablet.

"Normally you have to be twelve," Thea continued, "but he said I've improved so much lately, I'm ready to dance with the older group."

I nodded, half listening, as an image popped out at me. In it, a row of luminarias lit up a string of photos attached with clothespins to a bright red ribbon.

Idea-sparks started going off. We could hang a bunch of photos on the patio, and strings of lights, too. And the luminarias could be different colors, like a rainbow!

"Helloooo? Earth to Blaire! Are you even listening to me? This is BIG."

I looked up from the screen. "Sorry. That is amazing news. We should celebrate!"

"That's what I was saying. What if you come watch my dance rehearsal tomorrow and then we go to Trinkets afterward?" Thea pretended to push a shopping cart. "I got a gift card for my birthday," she sang.

Trinkets is our favorite store in town. "I'm in!" I said.

⁕

Tuesday morning, after the B and B breakfast service was done, Mom and I drove to the art store in town to buy supplies for Cat's proposal. I'd emailed Gabe my plans for the The Big Moment the night before and he'd given me the green light. I couldn't wait to start making the decorations.

Afterward, while Mom ran errands, I walked to the community center where Thea's dance troupe rehearsed. When I peered through the open door of the dance studio, I saw that Thea was right—the girls were all a couple of years older than us. But Thea was tall, and she fit right in. She looked so intense and focused as she moved to the lively Greek music. Advancing to the older group obviously meant a lot to her.

When class was over, Thea came out of the studio and flashed me a little smile.

"Bravo!" I said, giving her a mini round of applause. "You looked amazing!"

"Totally," said another girl who'd also been in class.

"Thanks, you guys," Thea said. "Blaire, do you know Madison? She's going into seventh grade. She had Ms. Burdick for fourth just like us."

I recognized Madison, but I'd never talked to her before. "Hi," I said, giving a little wave.

"So are you going to audition for the duet?" Madison asked Thea.

"There's going to be a featured dance at the fair this year," Thea explained to me. "It's kind of a big deal if you get it."

"You *have* to audition," I said. "You'd be great!"

"You should!" Madison agreed.

Thea nodded. "Thanks! I'll think about it."

"Hey," Madison said. "A few of us are going for milk shakes at Moxie Café. Do you guys want to come?"

I love Moxie Café, and I love the way Thea always does her pretend French accent when we order. But the thought of a milk shake made me panic. I pictured myself sitting there while everyone ordered ice cream and I stammered to explain why I wasn't getting any. It reminded me of Thea's party, and I sure didn't want to feel all awkward and embarrassed again.

"Come on, Blaire," Thea said. "Moxie has plenty of nondairy stuff, too. I'm sure you can find something you can eat."

I felt myself blush. Why did Thea always have to talk about my dairy issue? "Um, no, thanks," I said, trying to sound casual. "Go ahead. I forgot to buy some stuff at the art store anyway. Let's do Trinkets another day."

"You sure?" Thea asked.

I nodded. I watched Thea and the others cross the street and disappear around the corner. None of them would have to worry about rushing to the bathroom after drinking a milk shake. Just the thought of what that ice cream would do to me made my stomach turn over. I let out a big sigh. *This new normal is pretty lonely.*

CHAPTER 7

Please Say Yes

After six days of crafting and coordinating for Operation Sneaky Proposal, it was go time.

We picked Sunday evening because Cat would be gone all day at a farmers' market across the river. That gave Gabe a chance to help Beckett write and plant the notes, while Thea and I decorated the patio. Cat was due back at the farm by eight o'clock. Thea was desperate to stay, but she had to get home for a family dinner. "Remember every little detail," she said to me before she left, "so you can tell me tomorrow."

Beckett and I sat in front of the greenhouse, playing tic-tac-toe in the dirt, feeling as excited as if it were Christmas Eve. At three minutes after eight, Cat finally pulled up. "Hey, guys!" she called. "Are you here to help me unload the truck?"

"Even better," Beckett called, pointing at the door of the greenhouse. "We have a surprise for you!"

Cat saw the note taped to the door handle of the greenhouse. "What's this?"

"It's for your anniversary," I said.

"I have an anniversary?" asked Cat.

"Of working at Pleasant View Farm. It'll be two years this month."

Cat smiled. "Wow, you're right. Time flies." She pulled the note off the door and read it out loud:

"You love our farm and our farm loves you.
We got you a gift that's not green or blue.
Come to the barn so you can see
What this awesome thing will be!"

Cat tucked the note into her pocket and looked at us with a twinkle in her eye. "A game, huh? Okay, I'll play!"

Beckett and I exchanged a glance. So far, so good.

When we got to the barn, there was no gift in sight. Just Dad's tools spread out on his workbench.

"I'm getting the sense I'm going to have to work for this surprise," Cat said.

"I wonder what's up in the loft?" I asked in a sing-songy voice.

Cat scurried up the steps Dad recently built and found the note Beckett and Gabe had tacked to one of the beams. She leaned over the railing and began to read:

"Ha ha ha, sorry for the fakeout.
We'll make it up to you with some deli takeout.
Come see the chickens, they're standing guard.
Over a gift that waits for you in their yard."

Cat peered down at us and narrowed her eyes. "Did you name another chicken after me?"

I giggled. "Maybe."

As we walked past the herb garden to the coop, I looked up to find Gabe watching from a second-floor window of the house. I flapped my arms like chicken wings. That was our signal for "Everything's good."

When we got near the chicken coop, Dandelion and her friends clucked a symphony. It was like they knew what was happening and were thrilled to be part of it.

But the note that was supposed to be taped to the coop gate wasn't there. I looked at Beckett. Beckett looked at me and pinched his nose as if he was smelling something terrible. That was our signal for "We've got a problem!"

Uh-oh.

Cat opened the gate and searched the coop. "I'm assuming there's another note in here somewhere. Please don't tell me I have to look under the chickens."

"There it is!" cried Beckett, pointing to the white slip of paper lying on the ground in the corner of Penny and Dash's pen. "The wind must have blown it off the coop."

Oh, good.

But as soon as Cat approached the pen, Dash trotted over to greet her. That's when he noticed the paper, too. Now it was a race.

"Get it before Dash does!" I called to Cat as she scrambled through the gate and into the pen.

"Is this part of the game?" Cat called as she lunged at the paper. But Dash was faster, and in a second, the goat had the note in his mouth.

"Drop it!" I said as I tried to pull the paper out of Dash's mouth. I managed to rip a corner of it away from him, but he got most of it. He chewed slowly and then swallowed.

"Maaaaah!" Dash said. It sounded like *Delicious!*"

"Bad goat," Cat said, trying not to laugh. She looked over my shoulder as I straightened out the slip of paper. All that was left was the first line of the clue.

"Okay, so we had to prank you again," I read aloud.

"Good prank," Cat said.

"Beckett, what did the rest say?" I whispered.

"I don't remember," he whispered back. Then he pinched his nose again.

I tried to think, but my mind was blank. All I could remember was that we had to get Cat to the gazebo for her next clue. We couldn't give up the game and just tell her where to go next. It would ruin the magic.

I am the proposal assistant, I told myself. *I will make this work.*

"Okay, so we had to prank you again," I repeated. "We . . . we promise . . . this will, um . . . someday end," I stammered. "At the gazebo by the creek . . ."

Oh no. What rhymes with creek?

"You'll see this gift and out you'll freak!" Beckett finished.

Cat burst out laughing. "Nice save. To the gazebo!"

Of course, the game didn't end at the gazebo. There was another note sending her to one of the vegetable fields. And in the vegetable field, taped to a marker flag, there was a poem telling her to go to the porch of the house.

"I know where all this is headed," said Cat.

"You do?" Beckett and I said together.

"The restaurant, right?" she continued. "An extra large dish of crème brûlée?"

"Let's go see," I said, relieved that she hadn't figured it out.

When we got to the porch, she read the last clue taped to the rocking chair:

"You've made it this far, you're almost there.

We know we haven't been totally fair.

Come to the restaurant, your surprise does wait.

Hurry, hurry, you don't want to be late!"

"Aha!" Cat exclaimed. "I was right."

Beckett and I followed Cat through the house and into the restaurant dining room. It looked like any other Sunday evening, with tables full of guests. But tonight, Grandpa, Mom and Dad were standing at the far end of the room, in front of the French doors that led to the patio. My heart was pounding as Cat walked over to my parents. I was nervous. I could only imagine what Gabe was feeling on the other side of the doors.

Cat hugged my parents and grandpa. "Maggie . . . Daniel . . .and Ben! Thank you . . . I . . ."

"Not yet," said Mom.

"You have a little farther to go, " Dad added.

Cat tilted her head, confused, as Grandpa opened the patio doors.

There, on the courtyard patio, were dozens of pictures of Gabe and Cat smiling, laughing, and holding hands. Thea and I had strung the photos on rainbow-striped ribbons and hung them so that they crisscrossed the patio. Strings of tiny, multicolored lights added a soft glow to the evening sky, which was turning pink and purple with the sunset.

We had lined the stone tiles of the patio with luminarias that I'd made from the paper bags from Gabe's favorite deli. Cat laughed when she saw them. "I hope Gabe wasn't in charge of food for tonight."

"Follow the bags," I told Cat.

She did. When she got to the other side of the big oak tree, she gasped. There, in a circle of luminarias, were tiny white candles that spelled out: CAT, WILL YOU MARRY ME?

Gabe stepped out from around the corner, looking so nervous, I was afraid he wouldn't be able to speak. He didn't say a word. Instead, he got down on one knee and pulled a small box out of his pocket.

Cat took a step back. She didn't say anything either.

Aren't people supposed to talk during a proposal? What if this wasn't going like it was supposed to?!

Then Cat rushed toward Gabe and threw her arms around him, saying, "Yes, yes, yes!"

Mom and Dad and Grandpa and Beckett and I cheered.

"I didn't even have to do my speech!" Gabe laughed.

"You said it all, with this." Cat motioned to the photos, lights, candles, and lanterns.

Gabe met my eyes and mouthed the words *Thank you*.

"Good job, proposal assistant," Mom whispered to me before she went to get the crème brûlée. "You created a totally unique setting for this incredible memory."

I looked at Beckett. He looked at me. We both started flapping our arms.

CHAPTER 8

Impossible Invitations

The next morning, my tablet dinged before I even got out of bed.

> **Thea:** How did the proposal go last night????? 🖤🖤🖤🖤😊💍
>
> **Blaire:** SHE SAID YES! It was super romantic.

I added a GIF of a cute sheep holding a sign that read, WILL EWE MARRY ME?

> **Thea:** LOL! Yay! When's the wedding?
>
> **Blaire:** Don't know yet! They've only been engaged for, like, 12 hours. 😌
>
> **Thea:** Oh, right. 😄

Thea: Sabrina, Amadi, and I are going to see Zoo Adventures 3 later today. Want to come?

I hadn't seen Sabrina or Amadi since Thea's party, and I loved *Zoo Adventures 1* and *2*. I was about to type, *I'm there*, but I stopped. Nachos and cheese. That's what we always eat at the movie theater. If I went, I couldn't have any. After skipping last night's crème brûlée, I wasn't up for another reminder of what I was missing.

Blaire: No thanks.

I started typing more, to explain why I didn't want to come, but nothing I wrote sounded right. It was too much to explain in a text anyway. Delete, delete, delete.

Blaire: But maybe you can come over later and we can play with the animals?

Thea: OMG yes! I'll ask my mom.

Blaire: Awesome! She'd better say yes!
☝️

Later, when I went out to collect eggs, I saw Cat sitting in the porch swing. "Hey, bride," I said.

Cat jumped, and her phone flipped out of her hands. I caught it.

"Sprout! You startled me!"

"Sorry," I said, handing her phone back to her. "You okay?"

She nodded as I sat down next to her. But she didn't look okay. "Aren't you supposed to look happy after getting engaged?" I asked.

"I just got off the phone with my brother," Cat explained. "He was so excited about my news, but he had some news, too." She took a deep breath. "He's being deployed at the end of August. He doesn't know when he'll be back."

"Oh." I sighed. I knew how hard it was for Cat to be so far from Lorenzo.

"Ever since our dad died," she continued, "I've always imagined Lorenzo walking me down the aisle at my wedding. But that would mean we'd have to get married . . ." She flipped to the calendar on her phone. ". . . eight weeks from now. I don't mind doing it that soon, but there's no way we'll be able to make it work. Gabe has a huge family, and I'm sure any spot big enough for that many guests is already booked."

Cat and I sat in silence for a moment, listening to the chickens clucking, a mixer whirring in the kitchen, and Dad hammering in the barn.

"Cat, wait!" I said, because I'd just had the best idea-spark in the history of idea-sparks. "You should get married here! At Pleasant View! In the new barn!" I jumped off the swing.

Cat's face lit up brighter than all those candles at her proposal. "That would be perfect!" Then that brightness vanished. "But there's so much work left to do on the barn, there's no way it'll be ready before Lorenzo leaves."

"Not if Dad keeps working alone," I said. "But I could help him. Every day. And we could ask Gabe. And Grandpa. And—"

Wait a sec! If Cat got married in the barn this summer, her wedding would be our first big event. The event that decided whether Grandpa stayed or moved out! Cat was like another grandkid to Grandpa. He'd never leave because of her wedding.

"Cat, you *have* to get married in our barn," I said. "Let me talk to Mom and Dad."

Cat's eyes widened. "Seriously? It would mean so much to me to have the wedding here."

"You're family," I said.

Cat smiled and gave me a hug. "True. You're the closest thing I have to a little sister, Sprout, so there's something I'd like to ask you. Would you be my junior bridesmaid?"

A junior bridesmaid? I had no idea what I'd need to do, but I couldn't wait to find out!

I squealed, "Yes! Oh my gosh, yes!" I hugged Cat so tight, we both almost fell off the swing.

CHAPTER 9

Operation Barn Renovation

B y the end of August?" asked Dad.

"As in, two months from now?" added Mom.

We were sitting at a rickety round table in a room we call the Command Center. It used to be a small parlor on the first floor of the house, back when Grandpa was growing up, but over the years it turned into the Pleasant View Farm office.

"I wish we had the budget to hire a professional crew," Dad said. "But we don't. And I can't finish that fast by myself."

"You won't have to," I insisted. "I'll help. And we could ask Gabe. And maybe Grandpa can . . ."

"Maybe Grandpa can what?" asked Grandpa, coming into the room with a stack of papers.

In one long breath I said, "Help finish the barn so Cat can get married there in late summer so her brother can give her away before he gets deployed."

At the mention of Cat, Grandpa smiled. "I'm really happy for Cat and Gabe," he said.

I knew there was a "but" coming.

"But I want no part of the barn stuff," Grandpa continued. "It's a bad idea to begin with, and now you want to rush it? That sounds risky."

"Dad," said Mom to Grandpa, "you're assuming the worst. Cat's worked so hard for us. I'd like to make this happen for her." Then Mom turned to Dad. "Daniel, what do you think?"

Dad looked at me. "Are you sure you want to give up so much of your summer, Blaire? It will be a big commitment. You won't have much time with your friends."

Friends? Thea! "Thea could help, too!" I hadn't mentioned any of this to Thea yet, but she had helped with the proposal, so of course she would help with the wedding. I'd just have to remember to ask her when she came over later. "We'll do whatever needs to be done," I promised.

"Well, I've never regretted going after something challenging," Dad said. "Let's do it!"

Grandpa sighed. "This family has always voted on big farm decisions, and it seems I've just lost this one." He dropped his papers on the table and left.

"Don't worry about him," Mom said. "He'll come around. He always does."

I hoped she was right. I didn't want Grandpa to be unhappy. I definitely didn't want him to move out.

"Blaire, I know you're bursting to tell Cat the good news," Mom said.

I was!

I found her in the greenhouse. "Caaaaaatttt!" I shouted, breathless from running as fast as I could. "It's a yes!"

Cat was shocked. "Are you kidding? Really?"

"Really. So what kind of wedding do you want?" I asked, my heart still pounding. "During the day or at night? Fancy or casual?"

Cat held up her hand. "Whoa! Slow down. I haven't even told Gabe about this yet. That should be step one."

"Let me know when you're ready for step two—because we have only *two* months to go." I laughed. "Oh, and if you need some ideas for the wedding, I have, like, fifty billion of those."

"Of course you do," Cat said, pulling out her phone to call Gabe. "I'll keep that in mind."

꽃

That afternoon, Mrs. Dimitriou's car pulled into the driveway and out stepped Thea, wearing a big straw hat and holding a curved shepherd's crook with a bow on it. Of course.

"Can you believe I still have my Little Bo Peep costume from our first-grade class play?" Thea asked, waving the crook. "Now I'm ready for a day with Penny and Dash."

"You look awesome," I said, "but there's been a little change of plans. Instead of playing with the animals, we need to help my dad in the barn." I filled her in on Cat and Lorenzo and everything.

"This Bo Peep's not much of a builder," Thea said, taking off her hat. "Can we at least play with the animals afterward?"

"Totally," I said. "Come on, Dad's waiting for us. It'll be fun, I promise."

Two minutes later, we were standing in the barn with work gloves and safety goggles on.

"I feel like a cyborg in these," Thea said as she tapped the goggles, then turned to my dad. "Mis-ter Wil-son, we are wait-ing for your com-mand," she said in a robot voice, moving her arms stiffly.

Dad said, "Well, my official Barn Renovation Helpers, eventually we'll be putting in insulation, electrical wiring, and new wood panels, but first, we have to cover the interior walls with housewrap."

"House rap?" Thea asked. "You mean like this?" She struck a hip-hop pose and launched into a rap. "I'm the new barn in town and I'm here to say—"

Dad grinned. "No, Miss Thea-ter." That was his nickname for my dramatic friend. "House*wrap*," he explained, "as in a very strong paper material that will keep out rain, wind, and cold. You girls will hold up a sheet, and I'll staple it into the wall," Dad told us. "The three of us can get the lower areas done in no time."

At first it was fun. Dad's staple gun made a really satisfying sound every time a staple went into the wood, and the time went by quickly as Thea and I kept thinking up lyrics to the rap:

I'm the new barn in town and I'm here to say,
I'm gonna keep the rain and the cold away.

*You wanna have a wedding where it's warm
and cozy?*
Come party right here, everything will be rosy!

But by the time we were on the second wall, Thea
wasn't rapping anymore. She had a grumpy scowl on her
face, too. "Are you okay?" I asked.

"This is hard work," she said, rubbing her shoulder.
"Can we take a break and go see the animals?"

"Definitely," I said, "as soon as we finish this wall."

"That's okay," Dad said. "You girls have earned a
break."

Thea said "Yes!" at the exact moment I said "No!"

"Up to you," Dad said, shrugging. "I'll be right
back." He headed outside.

"Blaire!" Thea said the moment he was gone.
"We've been holding housewrap up forever. My arms
feel like they're going to fall off."

"I know," I said, "but we have to finish the barn so
we can have the best wedding ever, or Grandpa's going
to move out."

"Wait . . . what?!"

I filled her in on what he said at Freddy's.

"But you don't think he'll actually—"

"Shhhh!" I said, because I heard Dad coming back. "Just please keep helping me?" I whispered.

Thea sighed. "Fine." She helped me pick up another sheet of wrap.

As we kept working, a heavy feeling in the pit of my stomach grew stronger. This was only Day One of Operation Barn Renovation, and my crew was already getting cranky. *Will we get this barn ready in time?*

***

A horse dressed up as a flower girl. *Swipe.* Robotic sunflowers that stick in the grass and sing "Here Comes the Bride." Weird! (But also kind of awesome.) *Save.*

It was the next morning, and I was sitting alone at the kitchen table with my tablet, searching for "unique farm wedding ideas." Cat wasn't ready to start brainstorming, but I was!

Swipe. A bale of hay decked out with sparkly pillows and a cozy throw blanket. Cute! *Save.* I'd send the good ideas to Cat later.

Grandpa poked his head in. "Ah, there you are! I have to help a guest; would you mind watching the front desk for a while?"

"Can I bring my tablet?" I asked Grandpa. "I'm doing wedding research."

He frowned. "People come first, Blaire," Grandpa said.

"Yeah, okay." I put my tablet in the basket on the kitchen counter where Mom made us all put our devices during meals, then headed down the hallway, plopping into the office chair behind the desk.

I opened up our computer system to see if anyone was supposed to check in or out today.

Suddenly, a little window popped up to announce a new email to the Pleasant View Farm account. It was from someone named Josephine Vandegriff.

Vandegriff was Gabe's last name. Were they related? I couldn't resist finding out.

Dear Pleasant View Farm,

I'm hoping this email finds its way to your event planner. I am overjoyed at the news of my son Gabe's engagement to Caterina Minardi!!!!!! However, you can imagine my surprise when they told me the wedding would be scheduled so soon. Your farm sounds like a beautiful location, but two months to plan a wedding??????? I would like to offer my help. I already have some terrific ideas. For instance, I'm picturing colorful paper star lanterns all over the ceiling. Barns have big ceilings to fill up, yes? I look forward to discussing more suggestions with you.

Very very sincerely yours,

Josephine Vandegriff

Finally! Someone who was just as eager to get going on wedding planning as I was!

I knew from Cat that Gabe's mother lived in Manhattan and was involved in a lot of charity fundraisers. Maybe that's why she assumed we had an event planner here at the farm. Funny how she already had ideas for the barn decorations even though she'd never been to Pleasant View. Maybe she got idea-sparks, like I did.

Colorful paper star lanterns filling up the barn ceiling. I could see that.

I wasn't allowed to use the Pleasant View Farm email account—my parents had strict rules about who I could interact with online, and how. But it wasn't like I was emailing some random person from the internet. This was Gabe's mom, and Gabe was practically family! *Mom and Dad won't mind in this case,* I told myself. I typed a reply.

Dear Mrs. Vandegriff,

Thanks for writing. I love your idea of
paper star lanterns! We also have a lot
of butterflies on the farm. Maybe we could
have giant paper butterflies, too. What do you
think?

Sincerely,

Blaire Wilson

I sent it off, and the reply came a minute later.

Dear Blaire,

Why, yes. I see it!!!! I can't wait to talk
about these ideas some more. When are you
available for a phone meeting?????

> *Wait, what?* A phone meeting?
> I read her email again, then read mine. And it hit me:
> Mrs. Vandegriff thought *I* was the Pleasant View
> Farm event planner!

CHAPTER 10

The Event Planner

B eckett, it's your turn," Dad said at the dinner table that evening. "What was your Up?"

This was a game our family played—sharing the best and the worst things about our days.

"Feeding Penny with her bottle," Beckett replied proudly. "She only pulled me over twice!"

"What was your Down?" Mom asked.

Beckett's smile vanished. "Stepping in her poop right afterward."

We all laughed, Grandpa extra loudly. "My sister and I used to compete to see who could pick up the most poop," Grandpa said. "Good times!"

"Okay . . . that's enough poop talk at the dinner table," Dad said, turning to me. "Blaire, your turn."

I paused, thinking. I'd been planning to tell my parents about Mrs. Vandegriff. But was our email exchange an Up, because I was excited to trade wedding ideas with her? Or was it a Down because of the whole mistaken identity thing?

"My Up was . . . um . . ."

Suddenly there was a knock on the back door. Cat and Gabe stepped inside.

"Sorry to bother you guys," said Cat. "I was wondering if I could speak with the Pleasant View Farm event planner?"

Uh-oh.

"We don't have an event planner," Mom said, putting her fork down.

Cat just raised her eyebrows at me as she and Gabe took two empty chairs at our table.

"Blaire," Dad said, catching Cat's glance. "What's Cat talking about?"

"Um . . . well, I . . ." I gulped. "When I was at the desk this morning, an email showed up and I may have answered it."

"Blaire Wilson," said Mom, giving me a sharp look.

"I know I wasn't supposed to," I blurted out. "But Mrs. Vandegriff emailed Pleasant View looking for the event planner, and she had some good ideas, and we really should get started planning, and Gabe said she had a lot of experience organizing big fund-raisers—so I wrote back to her. I didn't mean for her to think I was the event planner!"

"Well, she did," said Gabe, a smiling a bit. "And she loved your ideas, too!"

"Really?" I asked Gabe.

But Mom, sitting next to him, still looked serious. "I'm concerned that you communicated with a stranger by email," she said to me, "and on an account that wasn't your own—"

"Mrs. Vandegriff isn't a stranger," I argued. "She's Gabe's mom—"

"Doesn't matter," Mom said. "*You* don't know her, which means she's a stranger, and strangers can be dangerous." She turned to Gabe. "No offense to your mom, of course."

"None taken, Mrs. Wilson," Gabe said. "You can never be too careful with this online stuff."

"This is serious, Blaire," Mom continued. "You know we—"

"*Mommm,*" I said, giving her a look to stop her speech. It was embarrassing to be chewed out in front of Cat and Gabe. "Can we stop talking about this now?"

"Yes," Mom said, her voice softening a little. "So long as you understand that going forward, you don't respond to any emails, on anyone's account, unless you've already met the person. Deal?"

I sat back in my chair. "Deal."

There was an awkward silence until Beckett said, "Can I change my Up?"

"I guess," Dad said.

"Blaire got in trouble!"

I kicked him under the table as Mom said, "That rule applies to you, too, buddy. Now, please clear the dishes, you two."

Beckett and I started gathering plates as Grandpa rose from his chair, too. "I hate to leave you all, but I told one of our guests I'd show them around the farm after dinner. If you'll excuse me."

Mom and I exchanged a glance. Was there really a guest waiting for a tour, or did Grandpa just not want to talk about wedding stuff?

"So," Gabe said after Grandpa left, "I'll explain everything to my mom. But she's going to be bummed that you're not the event planner."

Cat rolled her eyes. "He means that you would probably be much better dealing with his mom than me," she explained. "I can't talk flower arrangements or party decorations for very long."

"My mother can be a bit intense," Gabe said.

I was grabbing a glass off the table when an idea-spark suddenly burst in my brain. "Hold on," I said. "If Mrs. Vandegriff likes planning parties and I like planning parties, then maybe we could plan this party—I mean wedding—together."

Cat and Gabe exchanged a look. "I'd run everything by you two, of course," I promised.

"I have to say," said Cat, "you have a gift for making things special. I mean, what you did for Gabe's proposal was amazing."

"And that does sound like a perfect way to handle my mother," added Gabe.

"So that's a yes?" I asked.

"It is for me," Cat said. "But there are, uh, other people you have to ask." She pointed to Mom and Dad.

"Oh, right." I turned to my parents. "What do you think?"

"I have no doubt you can help plan a gorgeous wedding," Dad began, "but you're already pretty busy with the animals and helping renovate a gorgeous barn."

"*And* you're going to be a junior bridesmaid," added Mom.

"But I want to help Cat and Gabe make this special. It's like a dream come true! Please?" I scrunched up my nose the way I used to when I was little and wanted another cookie.

"Well." Mom sighed. "How can I vote no on a *dream come true*?"

"You have my vote, too, kiddo," said Dad. "But we meet every few days to go over what you're doing. Got it?"

"Yes, yes. Whatever you say!" I jumped up to hug him and then Mom. This was going to be SO. MUCH. FUN.

⚘

"Stop it. You're helping plan the wedding?" asked Thea from my tablet screen. I'd called her as soon as dinner was over. "I have just three words for you: O. M. G."

I laughed. "Yeah, that pretty much sums it up. But here's the thing: Will you help me? I'll need an assistant, especially at the wedding itself because I'll have brides-maid duties. Plus doing the proposal stuff with you was so much fun."

"It was," Thea said, a gleam in her eye. "Okay, I'm in—"

"Yes!" I said.

"But only if there aren't any more staple guns involved," she finished. "I never want to see one of those again in my life!"

I laughed. "Deal."

We said good-bye and hung up. It was getting kind of late, but there was an internet full of wedding ideas to be explored! I opened up my search window and dove in.

CHAPTER 11

Wedding Planning Is LIFE

07/09/2019

To: Cat Minardi

From: Blaire Wilson

Hey, Cat! I searched "farm wedding decorations" and found a ton of great ideas! I started an online inspiration board, <u>here's the link</u>. Take a look and let me know what you think. But don't take too long, I can't wait to get started! 😊

07/10/2019

To: Blaire Wilson

From: Cat Minardi

Wow, you're not kidding! There are a lot of options. I really like the weddings that have a rustic theme, where the decorations are inspired by nature. That fits the farm, don't you think? And it also fits me. I showed my favorite pictures to Gabe and he said whatever I want is fine with him, except he does have a short list of things he MUST have. Here's one: He'd like us to ride from the ceremony at the gazebo to the reception at the barn on an old two-person bike he's been working on. Can you come up with ideas to decorate it?

Mrs. V: Hello, event planner! Have you been able to pin Cat down on a direction for wedding decor? Clock's ticking!

Blaire: Hi, Mrs. V! Yup, I just heard back from Cat and she wants a rustic theme. Yay!

Mrs. V: Rustic? Oh dear, that's not what I was picturing. Rustic is for log cabins and tents in the woods. Not a wedding! Weddings should be fancy, even in a barn.

Blaire: Hmmm, I guess that's true. Okay, I'll tell her. 👌

07/12/2019

To: Blaire Wilson

From: Cat Minardi

Hey, Sprout, check out this photo of the farm at sunrise. I *told* you it was worth it to get up super early to help load the truck for the farmers' market. Don't you love the lavender streaks in the sky? That color is one of my favorites. Can we use that for the wedding?

Thanks for running interference with Mrs. V. I get that she wants fancy. That's who *she* is. Gabe thinks we can do both—rustic and fancy. What do you think?

07/12/2019

To: Cat Minardi

From: Blaire Wilson

Ooh, we could add some golden, coppery sort of color to the lavender. That would make things fancy. Hey—this wedding can be "farm fancy"! I'll let Mrs. V know.

You are on a ChitChat Hangout —↗+
with Thea, Amadi, and Sabrina

Thea: Hello?

Amadi: Yah, I'm here

Sabrina: Me too

Blaire: Me three! 😂 What's up?

Thea: Amadi and I are going to the town pool today, want to meet us there?

Sabrina: Yep, I'll ask my mom!

Blaire: Sounds fun!

Sabrina: I even have money for the ice cream truck this time, LOL. 🍦

Amadi: That's right, you owe me for that creamsicle! 😯

Thea: So Blaire, you're coming?

Thea: Blaire, are you still on?

Blaire: Yeah

Amadi: Can you come to the pool with us?

Sabrina: We haven't seen you since Thea's party, we miss you!

Blaire: Miss you, too. But I have work to do here on the barn and wedding. Next time, ok?

Thea: Really? Bummer. Sabs and Amadi, see you later!

Sabrina: Bye!

Amadi: Bye! 😎

Mrs. V: Farm fancy? Love it! Brava! What do you call those little pictures you put in your messages? Is there one for clapping hands?

Blaire: They're called emojis and you can find them on your keyboard! Here's the clapping hands one. 👏

Mrs. V: Oh my. Fun fun fun! Look at all these! 🍒 💄 🍩 🧚 🌵

Blaire: 🌵?

Mrs. V: It's cute! Oh my, I already have some good ideas for farm fancy. Cat and Gabe can leave the wedding in a horse-drawn wagon decorated in white silk!

Blaire: Oooh! I like it. And maybe the horses can be wearing unicorn horns. Because unicorns are way fancier than horses!

Mrs. V: Yes! 🦄 Look, now I've got it.

Blaire: LOL! I'll also send you a link to my online inspiration board. You can add stuff, too.

Mrs. V: Great, I will share some pics of floral arrangements. 😈

Blaire: Um, evil?

Mrs. V: What's evil?

Blaire: You sent a smiling devil face, so I thought . . .

Mrs. V: Is that what that is? I thought it was a purple cat! 😊

Mrs. V: That is not what I meant to send. I meant this one. 😳

🌿

Amadi: Hey Blaire. My family's having a barbecue potluck thing later. Thea and some other people will be there. Hope you'll come. You can bring a snack to share!

Mrs. V: Blaire, darling, how's it going today?

Blaire: Good! Just added some centerpieces to the inspiration board! Go check them out. I really like the ones that look like birds' nests with eggs in the middle—they remind me of the chickens here on the farm. But we can fancy them up with glitter and stuff!

Amadi: So you're bringing fancy eggs to the potluck? Can we eat glitter?

Blaire: OMG, I thought I was answering Gabe's mom. Sorry! Can't come to the potluck, but have fun!

07/15/2019

To: Blaire Wilson

From: Cat Minardi

Sprout! I just looked at the new stuff you added to the inspiration board. Some of this is cool but I think there's a lot more "fancy" than "farm" in here. Like the picture with the sequined silver fabric on all the chairs? I thought we were sticking to lavender and copper? By the way, I posted some photos of wildflowers that we have on the farm because I'd like to use those. But the photos are gone. Did you take them down?

Mom: Hi, Blaire.

Blaire: Hi Mom.

Mom: Oh good, I do still have a daughter named Blaire!

Blaire: LOL. Why are you texting me, you're in the next room.

Mom: This seems to be the only way I can get your attention. Can you come in here? Your dad and I would like to chat.

CHAPTER 12

Experiments

"Hey," I said to Mom and Dad, who were sitting on the couch in the living room. I waved at Grandpa, who was on the other side of the room reading the newspaper. He winked at me and went back to the Local section.

"Come sit," Dad said, pointing to a chair opposite them.

"You guys want a wedding planning check-in, right? I have lots of new ideas to show you." I pulled up my inspiration board and placed the tablet on the coffee table between us.

"Great," Mom replied, picking up my tablet. "But first, your dad and I are concerned about how you've been so absorbed in this device lately."

"I haven't been *that* absorbed," I said. "I've been helping Dad in the barn most of the time. And what I do online is for wedding stuff."

"We know. You're taking your job seriously, and we're proud of you for that. But you're spending way too much time by yourself, lost in a screen."

Across the room, Grandpa rustled his newspaper.

"That's where all the good ideas are," I protested.

Mom closed the tablet, then got up and put it on a shelf. "Well, let's give it a break for the night."

"Hey!" I begged, starting to get up.

"Not negotiable," she said in the firm voice I knew too well. I sat back down.

"Besides, that's not where the good ideas are," Dad said. "Last time I checked, they were all in here." He leaned over and tapped the top of my head.

"Well, okay," I said. "But isn't it a combo? Mom, don't you get inspiration from recipes you see online?"

"Sure, I do," Mom replied. "But just the inspiration. Then I take that and experiment in the real world. Try that, okay?"

"Fine." I sighed. "I'm going to go check on the animals."

It's not working! Why isn't it working?

I took Mom's suggestion, and the next afternoon I was doing some experimenting based on what I'd seen online: a delicate bird's nest centerpiece with fake moss and silver eggs inside it. But I figured why use fake moss when we had real moss handy? And if the eggs were covered in lavender and copper glitter, that would add Cat's colors and the "fancy" factor, right? I had gathered some moss along with twigs for the nest from the woods that morning. Eggs were courtesy of Dandelion and her friends.

But nowhere online did it say how hard it would be to wrangle twigs into a nest shape. My "nest" looked more like a raft, the eggshells kept cracking when I tried to paint on the glitter glue, and the moss was making everything all dirty.

Beckett came bounding out of the house onto the porch. "Ooooh!" he said, seeing my nest raft. "Are you making a fort?! Can I help?!" He leaned in closer to look at the eggs. "Is there supposed to be a worm there?"

"What?!" I leaned in, too. An earthworm was squiggling out from under one of the eggs—I must have picked it up with the moss this morning. "Yuck!"

Beckett picked up the worm and dangled it front of me. "Do you want it, or can I have it?"

"You can have it, Beckett," I said. He grinned and ran off. Good. I did *not* need my little brother around right now.

What I *did* need was my wedding assistant. I snapped some photos of the centerpiece and then texted Thea.

> **Blaire:** Hey, wedding assistant. I can't
> make these look the way I want. HELP!

I stared at the screen while waiting for Thea's reply. Where *was* she? We hadn't talked much lately, and she hadn't been back to help with the barn. I realized how much I missed her.

Finally, Thea messaged me back:

> **Thea:** Hi, what's up? Cool sparkly
> things. I'm sure you'll figure it out.

I waited for her to type more, offering advice. But that was it. No emojis or funny GIFs either. Was she mad at me?

> **Blaire:** What R U doing?

Half an hour later, she still hadn't replied. Maybe she'd missed my text. I sometimes missed short ones, too. I texted her a photo I'd taken of Penny the lamb with an adorable expression on her face. It actually looked like she was smiling! Pleasant View Farm had gotten a ton of likes online when we'd posted it.

> **Blaire:** Look at this face! Penny
> misses you!

No answer. I waited one minute, then two. After three minutes, I went back to working on my centerpieces but couldn't concentrate. It wasn't like Thea not to answer right away, especially for a super hilarious photo like that.

"Blaire!" called Mom from the restaurant kitchen. "I've got a surprise for you!"

I hopped up and dashed inside, bringing my tablet with me in case Thea texted. Mom was standing in the kitchen with a big grin, holding something behind her back.

"What is it?" I asked. "A magical cure for my lactose intolerance?"

"Sort of," she said. She held up the surprise. "Ta-da!" All I saw was a shrink-wrapped block of something white.

"Ohh-kay," I said, not sure what I was looking at.

"It's soy cheese!" Mom exclaimed.

"Ew," I said, scrunching up my nose.

"Hey now," Mom said. "You haven't even tried it yet." She put the block down on the counter. "I know you haven't wanted to cook lately since you can't have dairy. And I totally understand. But maybe you can start cooking with dairy *substitutes*."

I put the tablet down. "I don't know, Mom."

"You can start with something simple. How about a grilled cheese sandwich? It's one of your all-time favorites, and we'll just tweak it a little for the new, healthier Blaire."

Mmmm. Grilled cheese. I hadn't had one since long before that day in the doctor's office.

Mom grabbed a skillet from the pot rack. "How about this: I'll make a sandwich and we can split it."

"Will soy cheese cook up the same as regular cheese? Like, will it get all gooey?"

"I'm not sure," Mom replied. "Let's experiment!"

We got to work. Mom sliced the soy cheese, and I used olive oil to grease up the bread so it got crispy, the way I liked it. As Mom grilled the sandwich, my mouth started to water. When it was done, she put it on a plate and cut it in half. Cheese oozed out. That was a good sign!

Mom handed me my half and held up hers. We touched our sandwich halves together.

"To grilled soy cheese," I said, feeling hopeful.

I took a bite. Crispy bread, check. Warm gooeyness, check. But as I chewed, something wasn't right. The texture was rubbery, and it didn't taste like the cheese I loved. I tried not to think of the worm Beckett had found in the moss earlier.

Mom was chewing her bite slowly. "Hmmm," she said. "This is . . . sort of . . . a bit . . ."

I managed to swallow. "I think the word you're looking for is *gross.*" I dropped my half on the plate.

Mom put her sandwich down, too. "You're right. It's gross. Okay, so this experiment officially failed, but there are plenty of other substitutes out there." Mom put her arm around me. "We'll try again, okay?"

"Maybe," I said.

"I'll talk to the Martins," Mom said. "They'll have some ideas." Joan and Elliott Martin are our neighbors, and they run a dairy. Mom uses all their stuff in the restaurant. They have the best cheese ever.

I looked at the clock. "I've got some chickens to feed," I said, grabbing my tablet.

"And I have to make your brother a snack before I

get ready for the dinner service. Hey, Blaire," Mom said as I headed for the door.

"Yeah?"

"Thanks for trying with the cheese."

I grinned. "I don't think we should call that stuff cheese!"

Out at the coop, I told Dandelion about the experiment gone wrong. "It was a mess," I said. "But you know what? I liked cooking with Mom again—even if it was just a sandwich."

Dandy clucked sympathetically just as my tablet dinged. Finally, Thea answered!

> **Thea:** Adorable! 🖤 I haven't seen the animals in forever. Or you. Maybe I could come over for a sleepover tonight?
>
> **Blaire:** I was thinking the same thing! BFF jinx!

We sent high-five emojis back and forth like we always did when that happened. *Yes! This was the BFF I knew.*

> **Blaire:** Hey—do you have any glitter
> glue? I'm all out and we still need to
> figure out those centerpieces.

I waited while Thea typed. She took forever to reply.

> **Thea:** Actually, if I come over, maybe
> we could NOT do wedding stuff?

Huh? Thea hadn't actually done any wedding stuff with me since that day in the barn.

> **Thea:** I have this Epic Sleepover idea
> anyway—campout with Penny and
> Dash in the pen!! What do you think?

That was actually a really good idea—I wished I'd thought of it.

> **Blaire:** A sleepover with the animals?
> Genius! 💡 🙌 Let's do it!

My stomach started growling, so I headed back to the kitchen. My tablet dinged again right as I got inside. Another text from Thea, with a photo this time.

> **Thea:** Hey, remember this place?

It was a selfie of Thea in front of a waterfall. I would have recognized that swimming hole anywhere—it was Split Rock. Thea and I always tried to find the funniest possible way to jump off the rock into the water. So that's why she hadn't been replying. She was swimming. *Whew.*

Blaire: Split Rock! Good times!

Another photo came through. This one was of Madison, the girl from Thea's dance troupe, doing her own jump off the rock. Her legs were in cross-cross-applesauce, and she was leaning her elbows on her knees, like she was just hanging out there casually in midair.

Thea: Madison officially won the Funniest Jump Award today.

I felt my stomach drop. Thea played our game without me? She hadn't even told me she was going to Split Rock.

Thea: I'll show you more pics tonight when I come over.

Blaire: Sure.

I set my tablet down on the counter. There was a plate with half a grilled cheese sandwich—a *real* one made with the Martins' fabulous sharp cheddar. Mom must have made it for Beckett. And Beckett didn't finish it? Didn't he know how good he had it?!

One bite's not going to hurt, a little voice inside me whispered.

So I took one bite. It was totally, completely delicious.

I looked at the photo of Madison at Split Rock and took another bite of the sandwich. *Why didn't Thea invite me today?*

Another bite.

Before I knew it, I'd . . . um . . . eaten the whole sandwich.

"Blaire?" Grandpa called me from the front desk. "Can you set up the afternoon service?"

We offer tea, coffee, and cookies to the B and B guests every day at four o'clock.

"Yup," I called back, turning my tablet off.

As I set things up in the common room, my stomach started cramping. It hadn't done that in a while—I'd forgotten how intensely awful it felt.

Forty-five minutes later, I was in my room, curled up on my bed, feeling absolutely terrible. I was in no shape for a sleepover.

Blaire: Not feeling great. Rain check on the sleepover?

Thea: Are you okay?

Blaire: Yeah. But . . . I MAY have eaten some cheese.

I attached a GIF of a dog looking guilty.

Thea: Blaire! That's not funny!

Blaire: I know. I didn't mean to. It just happened.

Thea: Bummer, I was really looking forward to the sleepover. I missed you today at the swimming hole!

I didn't know what to say to that. She didn't exactly look like she missed me in those photos with Madison. Besides, *she* was the one who hadn't invited me! Now she was making me feel guilty about canceling the sleepover?! It wasn't like I made myself sick on purpose. I'd just forgotten what eating cheese did to me . . .

Thea: Blaire? Hellooooo?

I knew I should talk to my BFF, but where would I even start?

Blaire: I'm going to bed. Good night.

Thea: Okay. Feel better soon.

I tossed my tablet down on the bed, tears welling in my eyes. Grilled cheese was out of my life, and now it felt like my best friend was, too.

I picked up the tablet again and opened the web browser. There were a few new episodes of *Dress Quest*. I'd watched two episodes when there was a knock on my door.

It was Beckett. "Dad says dinner's ready."

Ugh. My stomach still hurt, and I didn't want to tell Dad what happened. "I had a late snack," I told Beckett. "Can you tell Dad I'm not hungry?"

Beckett shrugged and left. I went back to *Dress Quest*, watching one episode after another until I fell asleep.

CHAPTER 13

So Farm-Like

I was in the front porch swing the next morning, my stomach feeling better, when a car pulled up. It was fancier than what usually arrived at the farm—shiny and black with dark windows. I couldn't see who was inside.

The car stopped and the back door opened. A woman stepped out. She was wearing a pink dress with tiny white dots and gold-toned high heels. Her hair was jet black, so big and poufy that at first it looked like she was wearing a hat. Tied around her neck was a shimmery white silk scarf. The scarf was fastened with a rhinestone brooch in the shape of a smiling frog with long eyelashes and big red lips.

The lunch service had started, but most of our noontime guests were people from the area. I usually knew them by name. But I had no idea *what* to call this lady. Maybe she was lost.

Then Gabe climbed out of the car.

Wait. Mrs. Vandegriff? OMG! I jumped off the swing.

"Hey, Blaire!" Gabe called.

"Blaire? Where?" Mrs. Vandegriff turned to me as I came down the steps. She clasped one hand to her heart and the other to her mouth, gasping dramatically. *"The Blaire Wilson? She's a real person? She doesn't just live inside my phone, coming up with wonderful wedding ideas?"*

I hid a giggle. For some reason I'd expected Mrs. Vandegriff's voice to sound like Thea doing a British accent. But Gabe's mom didn't sound like that at all. "I can't believe you're finally here, Mrs. Vandegriff!" I said.

"Call me Mrs. V, you brilliant mini designer. Come here and give me a hug!"

Mrs. V's super-tight squeeze took my breath away.

"Sorry for the unexpected visit," Gabe said.

"I couldn't go another day without meeting you in person," said Mrs. V. "So I called the car service and, lickety-split, I was on my way out of the city."

"This is great," I said. "Cat's in the orchard."

"I'll go get her," Gabe said quickly.

I grinned. "And I'll give your mom the Pleasant View Farm grand tour. This way, please," I said to

Mrs. V as Gabe headed in the other direction. "Our tour starts in the herb and flower garden." I did my best tour guide impression—Thea would have been proud.

"We don't use any pesticides, so all of the flowers here are edible," I told her, picking an orange marigold petal and eating it. "We use them as garnish in the restaurant." I moved down the row so I could pick Mrs. V another flower to taste. But when I turned around, Mrs. V was already chewing on a plant she'd picked herself.

"It's . . . interesting," Mrs. V said, twisting her face up.

"Oh no!" I said when I saw the plant in her hand. "You can't eat that one!"

Mrs. V dropped the weed and looked alarmed.

"Well, you *can* eat it," I stammered. "It just doesn't taste very good. Hold on." I picked her some mint. "To cleanse your palate."

"Oh, thank you dear," Mrs. V said, putting the leaf in her mouth. "Mmm, minty fresh!"

"Doesn't get any fresher," I agreed. "Now, follow me."

Mrs. V teetered a bit as her fancy gold heels sunk into the soft soil, but she steadied herself on the dirt path that led to the barn.

"Oh my," she exclaimed. "This is certainly the 'farm' in our 'farm fancy' wedding, isn't it?"

"Yep. But just wait," I called, pointing to the barn. "The fancy's up ahead."

When we got there, I slid open the barn door and froze. There were stacks of lumber, a wheelbarrow full of stones, and towers of paint cans. Definitely not fancy.

But Mrs. V looked up at the cavernous ceiling and towering wooden beams and broke into a huge smile. "Oh, I can see the potential! Such a marvelous space. You're going to have so many wonderful events here— what FUN!"

I wanted to hug her. Maybe I could get her to talk to Grandpa!

From the barn, I led Mrs. V to the animals and introduced her to the chickens.

"That's a chicken?!" she said when I picked up Dandelion. "It looks like a feather boa with webbed feet."

"Would you like to hold her?" I asked, thrusting Dandy toward her.

"No, no, no, no, no, dear. Thank you. Poultry makes me nervous. But she's lovely."

"How do you feel about lambs?" I asked, waving her toward Penny and Dash's pen.

Mrs. V practically squealed. "Who can resist a sweet little lamb? They're so darling and gentle and—*omph!*"

Suddenly, Mrs. V fell over and landed with a thud on the ground. Before I could help Mrs. V up, Dash was climbing on her backside like it was the summit of a mountain.

Maaaaaah!

"I see you have a goat, too," Mrs. V sputtered.

"Oh my gosh, I'm *so* sorry," I said, plucking Dash off Mrs. V. "The gate must have been open. Are you all right?"

Mrs. V stood and brushed herself off as I put Dash and Penny back in their pen. "I'm fine." She laughed. "More surprised than anything."

One of Mrs. V's shoes was lying on the ground. When I picked it up, the heel stayed stuck in the grass.

"Oh! It's broken," I said.

"No worries, I can get it fixed in the city," Mrs. V assured me. "I don't know what I was thinking with these shoes. I guess I didn't expect your farm to be so . . . farm-like."

"Do you need to take a rest?" I asked.

Mrs. V put her shoe back on. "Nonsense. I'm not that easy to get rid of. Onward!"

Mrs. V limped through the strawberry field, the blueberry patch, and the kitchen gardens. I pointed out the greenhouse in the distance and paused by the arch at the entrance to the orchard.

"I have one more spot to show you," I said, and led her through the orchard to the creek. We stopped at the edge of the wide, green lawn in front of the gazebo. Mrs. V took off her broken shoe and rubbed her ankle, balancing on her other foot.

"This is where Cat and Gabe want to have the ceremony," I said, holding a hand out to steady her. "They'll exchange vows in the gazebo, and we'll set up chairs on this lawn with an aisle going down the middle."

Just then, Beckett came rushing over. His pants were sopping wet and he held his hands cupped together like a little box. "I found the coolest thing in the creek!" he said.

"You also left Dash and Penny's gate open," I said. "And Dash's ball lying around. Gabe's mom tripped, and Dash jumped on her."

Beckett took in Mrs. V's bright pink suit and her awkward, one-legged stance. "You're Gabe's mom?" he asked. "You look like a flamingo."

"Don't mind him," I said, clapping my hand over his mouth. "He's seven."

Mrs. V smiled and put her broken shoe back on.

"That's okay. Gabe was seven once. What do you have there, young man? Something pretty? A beautiful rock?"

"Better than a rock!" said Beckett after I took my hand away. "Look."

He opened his hands and held up a frog.

A *dead* frog.

Beckett wiggled it around like it was dancing a jig. "Isn't it awesome?" he squealed.

Mrs. V stumbled backward in surprise. "Oh. Well. That's . . ." she stammered.

This tour was now officially a disaster. Would Mrs. V insist Gabe have the wedding somewhere else? "There won't be any dead frogs at the ceremony," I said. "I promise."

Mrs. V broke out laughing. "I've always liked frogs," she said, pointing to her brooch. "Perhaps each wedding guest could get one as a party favor!"

Beckett's eyes widened. "A dead frog? That. Would. Be. Awesome!"

"Ewww, Beckett. Gross!" I pointed to the creek. "Get that thing out of here!"

Beckett left, and I turned to Mrs. V. We both started laughing. "I guess we could put the frogs in little jars and tie pretty bows around them," I said.

"It would be—" Mrs. V started.

"Farm fancy!" I finished. "Let's head back to the house."

We were still giggling when we walked up to the front porch. Cat, Gabe, and my parents were waiting. When Cat saw us arm in arm, she broke into a big grin.

"Hello, my dear Caterina!" said Mrs. V, giving Cat a super tight hug. When Cat introduced my parents, Mrs. V gave them each her signature squeeze, too.

"It's wonderful to finally meet you," said Mom, eyeing Mrs. V's broken shoe.

"What do you think of Pleasant View Farm?" asked Dad.

"It's charming," said Mrs. V. "And so is Blaire."

Mom smiled. "Please, come inside for something cool to drink."

Suddenly I had an idea-spark. "We were supposed to have a wedding meeting tomorrow," I said, turning to Cat and Gabe. "But maybe we could do it now so that Mrs. V could join us?"

Mrs. V clapped her hands. "A wedding meeting! That sounds wonderfully official!"

While Mrs. V went to freshen up, I raced upstairs to

get my tablet. I changed into my favorite white sundress with little bumblebees on it, too, for good luck.

This is it! This is the first time Cat and Gabe are seeing all the ideas together. Will they love them as much as I do?

I was about to find out.

CHAPTER 14

Not Romantic at All

I'm so excited . . ." said Mrs. V. "I have goose bumps on my goose bumps!"

We were all sitting at a big table on the restaurant patio: Cat, Gabe, Dad, Mrs. V, and me. I propped up my tablet, and Dad had his laptop open with the budget spreadsheet he was working on.

I started with my ideas for the ceremony at the gazebo, swiping through photos on my online inspiration board. There were images of gazebos covered in a rainbow of colored tulle fabric, strung with twinkly lights and decorated with huge paper butterflies.

"What's that?" Cat asked, pointing at a picture of a pinwheel.

"I thought we could line the path to the barn with pinwheels," I explained. "They would look neat spinning in the sun."

Cat opened her mouth to say something, but Mrs. V interrupted.

"That reminds me," Mrs. V said. "I had a brainstorm when we were at the gazebo earlier. We need a red carpet down the aisle. Gabe's father and I owned the Carpet Queen store chain, and we always put a red carpet out in the parking lot for grand openings. Everyone felt like royalty."

Cat looked at Gabe.

"Um, Mom?" he said. "That's great for a grand opening, but maybe not a wedding."

"Fine, fine. Just an idea. Plenty more in here," Mrs. V said, tapping the screen of my tablet. "But we *must* have a bubble machine. We always had them at our big sales at Carpet Queen—remember, Gabe? When you were little, you liked to eat the bubbles. Anyway, they were my husband's favorite thing. A bubble machine will make it feel as if he's here at the wedding, too."

"Great idea," I said, grinning at Mrs. V. "It would be so fun to walk through a cloud of bubbles!"

"Just as long as Gabe doesn't eat them," Cat teased.

"Okay, now the reception," I said. I showed them more rainbow tulle, this time wrapped all the way up each of the barn's wooden posts. The place cards would be origami fortune-tellers made out of "rustic" brown paper, and the wedding favors would be packets of seeds that read LET LOVE GROW! in shimmery ink. In the corner of the barn, on a stack of hay bales, we would put a chicken nesting box where people could put their cards for Cat and Gabe. "I'll paint it sparkly lavender with 'Gabe and Cat's Nest Egg' in gold letters on the top," I explained. "The 'nest egg' part was Mrs. V's idea."

Mrs. V grinned.

I showed them my ideas for table decorations. "Check out these sparkly, floating gold candles I found," I said to Cat. "We can put them on all the tables in bowls with stones and water from the creek, with more tulle and some twigs, and the wildflowers from the field that you like. What do you think?"

There was a long pause. Finally, Cat said, "Whoa."

"Is that good?" I asked. "Do you love it?"

Cat glanced at Gabe, then leaned back heavily in her chair.

"Sprout," she began. "You have so many fun ideas. It's a lot to take in."

My heart sank. *She hates it.*

"It *should* be a lot," said Mrs. V. "Caterina, this is a wedding. Weddings are supposed to be big!"

"Not if you don't have the budget for it," Cat replied. She pulled Dad's laptop toward her and quickly looked over the spreadsheet, shaking her head. "We can't spend this much."

So it's not the ideas? I wondered. *It's the cost?*

"I can fix that, piece of cake!" exclaimed Mrs. V, snapping her fingers. "I'll cover whatever you can't."

"Oh no," Cat stammered. "I didn't mean to suggest that. I just want to keep things simple. More farm. Less fancy."

"I can do less fancy," I said. "What if we—"

"Wait," Gabe interrupted. "I like some of the fancy. Those gold candles are nice."

Cat looked at the spreadsheet. "Gabe, those gold candles are expensive."

"Consider them my gift to you," Mrs. V chimed in.

Gabe smiled. Cat looked away. The patio fell silent.

"I . . . I think I'll go for a walk," Cat finally said. She got up and left the patio.

My stomach dropped. *What just happened?*

Gabe got up and motioned for his mom to do the same. "Don't worry, Blaire," he said to me. "We'll get it all figured out."

Mrs. V gave me a tight hug. "I'll text you later," she said.

When they were gone, I turned to Dad. "Did I do something wrong?"

Dad shook his head. "No, sweetheart. You did great. Cat and Gabe are still figuring out what they want. You've been thinking about all these ideas for a while now, but this was the first time they've seen everything together." He picked up his laptop. "Let's put the planning on hold for a day or so, okay?"

"Okay." I sighed.

Wedding planning, it turned out, wasn't romantic *at all.*

CHAPTER 15

Cropped Out

I woke up the next day feeling so bummed about wedding planning being on hold that I stayed in my room all morning, playing games on my tablet. But after lunch, Grandpa insisted I come outside. "I need help with my project for the website," he said. I followed him to the animals' pen.

"Blaire, hop up on the fence right there," Grandpa said. "Okay, now Beckett, you kneel down in front of her with your arms around Penelope. Right! Just like that!"

Grandpa took a shot of us with his camera, then compared what he saw on the display with an old black-and-white photograph in his hand. "Pretty good match!" he said.

Beckett and I gathered around so we could see, too. The first photo was taken over sixty years ago, of Grandpa at age twelve, with his younger sister and one of their lambs. Then there was my brother and me, in the same pose in the same spot.

"That's so cool!" I said.

Grandpa was working on a new page for our website about the history of Pleasant View Farm. Our story started when my great-grandparents bought the land with the house and orchard and turned the surrounding fields into a working farm. Later, my grandparents renovated the rooms on the second floor of the house and opened the B and B. Finally, Mom made her dream of running her own farm-to-table restaurant come true by adding a commercial kitchen and a big dining space to the house.

"What are you going to do with the pictures?" Beckett asked.

Grandpa waved the old photo in his hand. "I'll post this one, along with the one I just took of you two, side by side, so folks can see Pleasant View 'then' and Pleasant View 'now.'"

Idea-spark! "The barn will be finished soon," I said. "Maybe you can take pictures of the new 'now' for that, too!"

Grandpa shook his head. "I wonder what my parents would say if they saw their old barn turned into a party space."

"I bet they would be happy we created a place for people to spend time with their family and friends," I said.

All Grandpa said was, "Mmm-hmm."

"And they'd like the bubble machine," I said eagerly. "Mrs. V is bringing one so that her dead husband can be at the wedding."

Grandpa stopped. "She keeps his remains in a bubble machine?"

I laughed. "L-O-L, Grandpa! No, I mean, having bubbles at events was something they both thought was fun."

"Okeydokey." Grandpa shrugged. "Whatever blows your bubbles, I suppose."

Beckett started laughing at something on the camera.

"Penny is totally *pooping* in this picture!" he said. "The one we just took!"

"What?" I craned my neck to see. Beckett was right. "Grandpa, we need to retake that shot."

"Nah, we can just crop that part out," Grandpa said. "Okay, next photo. Who's in the mood to climb some apple trees?"

"Me!" Beckett cried as he took off toward the orchard.

"How's Thea these days?" Grandpa asked as we followed Beckett. "I haven't seen her around the farm in a while."

I hesitated, not sure what to tell him. I wasn't even sure myself what was going on with me and Thea. "I guess we're both busy with other things this summer," I said finally. "But maybe that's how she wants it. The last time I talked to her, it didn't seem like she missed me at all."

Grandpa stopped. "What do you mean?"

We were at the arch at the entrance to the orchard. Beckett scrambled up an apple tree bursting with white blossoms. I told Grandpa about the swimming hole photos.

"A photo is just a photo, Blaire. One moment in time. It doesn't tell the whole story about Thea's summer or even that day." Grandpa paused, but I didn't say anything so he kept going. "Just like how that cropped photo we'll post doesn't tell the whole story of how cute baby animals sometimes involve not-so-cute stuff—like poop!" He smiled.

I tried to smile back. "I guess." Maybe the swimming hole trip wasn't what I thought it was. The photo couldn't tell me whose idea it had been. Maybe it was Madison who invited Thea, not the other way around, like I'd been assuming.

When we got back to the house, I found my tablet and texted Thea.

> **Blaire:** Hey! What's up?
>
> **Thea:** Nothing. Are you feeling better?
>
> **Blaire:** Yes! Hey, did you ever make it to Trinkets? 😯
>
> **Thea:** Nope not yet . . .
>
> **Blaire:** Let's go! Maybe Moxie Cafe, too.
>
> **Thea:** YEEEEEES! 😃 Saturday?
>
> **Blaire:** Yes! Yay! 👋 See you then. Can't wait!

Success! My tablet buzzed with another text. This one was from Mrs. V.

> **Mrs. V:** Hello, my dear Blaire!
>
> **Blaire:** Hi Mrs. V.
>
> **Mrs. V:** Superb news! Don't worry about Caterina wanting to drop some of our big ideas!!!!! 💡 Keep them all. I worked it out!!!! 😃 😃 😃
>
> **Blaire:** Really? That's great news! 🎉

Mrs. V: So full steam ahead! I can start ordering everything we need if you send me a list. All those thingies and whatchamajigs you showed us.

Blaire: And don't forget the dead frogs. 🐸 🐸

Mrs. V: Hee hee!!!! Of course!

Blaire: Or maybe not. Beckett would probably end up putting one down Cat's dress at the reception!

Mrs. V: I'll keep my eye on him. 😉 I can't wait to see Cat's dress!!! What does it look like?

Blaire: Oh, don't think she has one yet.

Mrs. V: What?! There's so little time!!! ⏰

Blaire: Yeah, she better get on that. I'll send you that list of supplies to order ASAP.

Mrs. V: Huzzah! Here we go! 😫

Mrs. V: Oops. I meant this one: 😍

Excellent. Wedding planning was back on. Thea and I had plans for Saturday. I flapped my arms like chicken wings. *Everything's good!*

⚜

That night after dinner, I was in the kitchen with my tablet, making lists for Mrs. V, when Cat came in holding her phone out in front of her. "Blaire's right here, Josephine," she said to the phone.

"What's up?" I asked Cat, confused.

"Mrs. V is video calling."

"Oh, great," I said. "She learned how to do that!"

Cat sat down next to me and held the phone out so that we were both in the frame. The only part of Mrs. V that was visible, though, was her ear. "Can you see me?" she asked.

"Hold the phone out in front of your face," I said.

"Blaire, is that you?" Mrs. V's face finally appeared on the screen. "Girls, I'm calling because a little birdie told me that Cat doesn't have her wedding gown yet."

Cat gave me a sideways glance. *Uh-oh*—maybe Cat didn't want Mrs. V to know she didn't have a dress yet.

"So," Mrs. V continued. "I've booked an appointment for Cat at Kellenberger's. You'll have a great selection of dresses and can find the perfect wedding gown!"

"No way!" I burst out. "Kellenberger's, like on *Dress Quest*?!"

Mrs. V laughed. "The very same one."

OMG. I imagined the store with its big chandeliers, fancy furniture, and walls of wedding gowns. Then I thought of Cat walking in as the bride. "You're so lucky, Cat."

"Josephine, thank you," began Cat. "You've been so generous. But I think Kellenberger's is much too fancy for me. I was planning on checking out a vintage dress shop—"

"Vintage?" said Mrs. V. "Well, if that's what you like, I'm sure Kellenberger's has plenty of new dresses that were carefully designed to look old!"

I couldn't believe Cat was passing up a chance to go to Kellenberger's. "Cat," I said, bouncing in my seat. "You *have* to go. It's *Kellenberger's*. It'll be super fun!"

Cat thought for a moment. "Okay. I'm game . . . but only if you come, too."

"Brilliant idea!" said Mrs. V. "We'll make a girls day of it! This Saturday."

OMG OMG OMG! Me? At Kellenberger's? Thea would positively *freak out* when I told her!

Oh no. Thea. Saturday.

I gestured to Cat and she lowered the phone so Mrs. V couldn't see us.

"Hello?" asked Mrs. V from the table. "Where did you go?"

"I have plans with Thea on Saturday," I whispered to Cat.

"Can you change them?" Cat whispered back. "I don't think I can do this without you."

Cat needed me? That settled it. "Thea will understand," I whispered.

Cat brought the phone, and Mrs. V on the screen, back up to my face. "We're in!" I said.

After Cat left, I texted Thea.

> **Blaire:** So guess what? Cat is going to Kellenberger's to shop for a dress! 👧
>
> **Thea:** No way! Jealous! Aren't you sooooo jealous?!?!
>
> **Blaire:** Actually . . . they asked if I'd go with them.
>
> **Thea:** Shut up! You're going, right?!

Blaire: Yeah. But it's on Saturday. What about our plans?

I waited as Thea typed. It took her a really long time to finally answer.

Thea: You should go. Have fun.

Blaire: Thanks—we'll go to Trinkets and Moxie Cafe another time. Promise.

I added a GIF of two cartoon monkeys with their hands locked in a pinkie promise.

Thea: Okay. Good night.

I waited for Thea to send me a funny GIF back. But nothing came.

CHAPTER 16

Dress Quest

I felt like a celebrity stepping out of the taxi at Kellenberger's.

Strangers hurried by on the Midtown Manhattan sidewalk. The frenzy of energy and movement was so different from even the busiest day at Pleasant View Farm.

"You've arrived!" shouted Mrs. V, who was waiting for Cat and me in front of the store. She was wearing a turquoise pantsuit and matching hat, with a rhinestone pin on her lapel that read MOTHER OF THE GROOM. "This is so exciting," she gushed, ushering us inside.

After we checked in at the front desk, a receptionist showed us to a waiting area. "Make yourselves comfortable," she said with a smile. "Your consultant will be here in a moment."

Cat and I settled down on a plush gray sofa. We looked at each other and immediately started giggling. "I can't believe I'm here," Cat said.

"Me neither," I said. I picked up a copy of *Empire State Weddings* magazine and started flipping through the pages. I stopped at a photo of a bride and groom in front of a barn sort of like ours.

"Cat, look," I said, showing her the picture. Mrs. V leaned over to see, too. "Maybe the Barn at Pleasant View will be in here someday!"

"Maybe." Cat smiled. "That would be something to see."

A moment later, a woman dressed in black introduced herself as Monique. She clearly knew Mrs. V, because Mrs. V gave her one of her death-grip hugs. "Let's see those gowns!" Mrs. V said.

"What gowns?" asked Cat. "I haven't picked any out yet."

"I stopped in yesterday and chose a few for you to start with," said Mrs. V.

"Oh. I see," Cat said. As we followed Monique down a long hallway, Cat leaned close to me and whispered, "No photos unless I say so, Sprout. Who knows what Mrs. V picked out."

Monique opened the door to a room full of silk, lace, taffeta, sequins, beads, and feathers. Cat seemed afraid to approach the dresses. "Oh gosh," she murmured.

"I know there's a wide range of styles here, Caterina," Mrs. V explained, "but that's part of the adventure. You never know which dress might make you say YES!"

"This is just a start," Monique added. "Once I know what your taste is, I'll be happy to find other gowns."

"It'll be fun," I assured Cat. "Like trying on costumes for Halloween."

Cat followed Monique into the dressing room. Mrs. V and I settled on a bench across from a half circle of mirrors. It seemed like forever before Cat finally came out. She was wearing a white silk dress with an enormous hoop skirt. She had to tilt the hoop up and shuffle sideways to get through the dressing room door.

Mrs. V drew in her breath. "Oh, how lovely!"

Cat's expression said, "Oh, how awful."

"Um, Mrs. V?" I said, "I think that skirt is bigger than the gazebo. If Cat wears that, there won't be room for Gabe at the ceremony."

"Good point, dear. Next dress."

The second dress had a narrower skirt, but the bottom of the hem was a circle of feathers. There were feathers at the scooped neckline and the elbow-length sleeves, too.

"Now, that makes a statement!" said Mrs. V. "And you must admit it's perfect for a country wedding."

But as Cat climbed up on the platform, she met my eye and gave a small shake of her head.

"You . . . um . . . look like a Silkie chicken," I said.

"That's a problem," Cat said, climbing off the platform. "I don't want to look like Dandelion on my wedding day."

The next dress, a one-shoulder gown that was covered in a million tiny beads and crystals, was clearly Mrs. V's favorite. "Oh, Cat. What a lovely bride you are."

Cat's smile was genuine. "Thank you."

"You're so sparkly!" I said.

"Is this one a maybe?" Mrs. V asked hopefully.

"Well, not *this* one," Cat said. "All these beads feel too fancy for me, and I don't really care for the one-shoulder look." She turned to Monique. "Do you have one with lace?"

"Oh, yes!" Mrs. V squealed. "There's a lovely lace option in there."

It was a long time before Cat came out again. When she did, she was wearing a strapless dress that was snug against her hips and legs and flared out at the bottom around her feet. "Monique tells me this is a mermaid style," Cat said, shuffling over to the platform. She could barely move her legs to walk. With Monique's help, Cat made it up the small step. Then she just stared at herself in the mirror.

"What do you think, Cat?" Mrs. V asked. "Do you like the lace?"

After a long pause, Cat finally said, "Yes. But I don't think I'm the mermaid type."

Mrs. V looked disappointed.

"Gabe is planning on them riding a two-person bike from the gazebo to the barn," I reminded Mrs. V as Cat shuffled back into the dressing room. "Cat wouldn't be able to pedal in that dress. And mermaid doesn't really go with 'farm fancy.'"

"You're right, I guess," said Mrs. V with a sigh. "It didn't look quite so fishy on the hanger. Oh dear, I'm not sure Cat's enjoying this."

"I think she is," I reassured Mrs. V. "Cat doesn't dress up that often. She just needs to get used to seeing herself in something other than work clothes."

"Hmmm," Mrs. V said. "Blaire, you may be onto something."

The next time Cat came out of the dressing room, she was wearing a sleeveless white satin dress with a wide band of beading around the waist. The style was simple, and Cat was beaming.

"I'm sorry, Cat," Mrs. V said quickly. "I picked that one before I knew how you felt about beads."

But Cat shook her head. "No—I like this," she said. Cat stepped up on the platform, and Monique adjusted the skirt so that the short train settled behind Cat in a gentle flutter.

"What do you think?" Cat asked, meeting my eye in the mirror.

I smiled. "You look perfect."

Cat smiled too. "Josephine?" she asked. "Do *you* like it?"

"Well, it's rather subdued, but it certainly suits you, Cat."

I squealed. "Cat! Is this THE dress? Have you ended your quest?"

"I do like it." Cat smiled and turned to Monique. "How much does it cost?"

When Monique told her, Cat's smile disappeared. "Whoa. That's just too much. I'll need to look at something in a lower price range."

Monique nodded. "Of course. Now that I know what you like, I'll go get some others."

As soon as Monique left, Mrs. V said, "Cat, if you love it, let's buy it! Consider it my gift."

"That's so kind, Josephine, but I can't. I would *never* spend this much on a dress I'm going to wear once."

"But it's your *wedding*, Cat, and—"

"Yes. It's *my* wedding, and I know what I'm comfortable with." Cat's voice was firm. "This dress is beautiful, but it's too expensive."

With that, Cat got off the platform and hurried into the dressing room. Mrs. V was absorbed with picking imaginary lint off her pantsuit.

Idea-spark. "Mrs. V, do they sell dresses for mothers of the groom here?"

She looked up and smiled. "They do."

"Maybe we should go look at them for a bit and give Cat some time to look at dresses by herself," I suggested.

Mrs. V agreed, so I tapped on the door to Cat's dressing room. "It's me," I called softly.

Cat opened the door and waved me in. She was still wearing the satin dress. When I told Cat where I was going, her shoulders relaxed. "Thanks, Sprout. I owe you."

An hour later, Cat and I said good-bye to Mrs. V outside Kellenberger's and watched her get into a cab. She was carrying a giant dress box. Mrs. V had purchased a dress for the wedding, but Cat had not.

On the train ride home, Cat leaned her head against the seat as we chugged along the Hudson River.

"Phew," she said. "I'm exhausted."

"Yeah, me too." I swallowed hard. "I'm sorry you didn't find anything."

"It's okay," Cat said. She offered me a quick smile as her phone chimed with a text message.

She spent some time messaging back and forth with someone while I stared out the window. Eventually, Cat fell asleep, her phone still in her hand. I didn't want her to drop it, so I pulled it gently out of her grip. Just as I put it down on the seat in between us, a new text message popped up on the screen.

> **Shannon:** Please don't say that, Cat. You CAN do this. Don't think for a second about calling off the wedding.

WHAT?!

I blinked a few times, trying to make sure I was reading that message right.

But there it was in bright, glowing letters. Cat must have told her friend Shannon about her frustrating day dress shopping with her future mother-in-law. Was Cat having doubts about the rest of the wedding plans? Would she really call things off? My stomach did a flip-flop.

This wedding was going to be one of a kind. It was going to make Cat so happy, and Grandpa, too.

I'd just have to work harder to make sure Cat could see that for herself.

CHAPTER 17

Fairly Disappointing

Mrs. V: Blaire!!! HUGE problem!! You know how Cat wants crème brûlée instead of a wedding cake???? My sister just called to remind me that her whole family can't eat dairy!! 🐷 🤢 What are we going to do?!

Blaire: No worries, Mrs. V! I'll talk to Mom.

Mrs. V: Oh, okay! So you'll have a dairy-free dessert option?

Would we? I thought it was just me who was going to have to skip the crème brûlée that night. But I guess if our guests had dietary restrictions, too, we needed a plan B.

Blaire: We'll figure something out.

Mrs. V: You are, as always, my hero.
♥♥♥♥👍😘😘😘

I went inside and found Mom in the restaurant kitchen. When I gave her the news, she didn't seem worried.

"Actually," she said, "I've been researching crème brûlée recipes that use coconut milk instead of cream."

"Is that even a thing?" I asked her. "Coconut milk crème brûlée?"

"*Definitely* a thing," Mom said, She brought up a few recipes on her laptop. "See?"

I stared at the photo on the screen. It didn't look any different from regular crème brûlée. Then again, that grilled soy sandwich had looked like the real thing, too.

"I have the ingredients we need," Mom said. "And I have time to test some recipes now if you want."

"Can you just do it?" I hadn't cooked since the Grilled Cheese Disaster.

"I can," Mom said. "But do you really want to avoid

cooking forever?" When I didn't answer, Mom added, "It would mean a lot to Cat if you made her favorite dessert."

I took a deep breath. That was true. "Okay," I said. "Let's get to work."

We spent the afternoon making three different versions of dairy-free crème brûlée. It was really fun to be experimenting with Mom again, tasting as we went. I realized how much time we used to spend cooking—and how much I missed it.

I'd just put a third recipe try on the stove when Grandpa came to find me, the phone in his hand. "Thea on the line for you," he said.

"Hi!" I said after I took the phone, motioning for Grandpa to watch the pot on the stove while I talked to Thea. Mom had gone to find something in the walk-in refrigerator.

"Hey," Thea said. "Just making sure we're still on for the fair tomorrow."

OMG, the fair! I'd totally forgotten it was tomorrow. We hadn't really talked about it lately. "Um . . . yeah," I said, as Grandpa snuck a taste from one of the finished crème brûlées on the counter. "Of course."

"Okay, good, Thea said. "When do you want to

meet? My dance troupe goes onstage at the International Pavilion at one o'clock."

"So I'll come watch your performance," I said as Grandpa tried the second crème brûlée. "Then afterward we can go on rides and see stuff." Grandpa shook his head. I wasn't surprised—that recipe definitely needed work.

"Make sure to get a seat up front," Thea said. "I'm excited because—"

I glanced at the third try on the stove, which Grandpa was supposed to be watching. It was about to boil over into a huge mess! I dashed over and turned down the burner.

"I wanted to tell you—" Thea was saying in my ear.

"Gotta go!" I said. "Wedding recipe emergency! Tell me tomorrow in person."

✳

The next afternoon, Dad, Beckett, and I drove to the fair. The guys were having a "Dudes Day" while I hung out with Thea. When Dad gave me my admission wristband, he also handed me Mom's phone. "In case you need to reach me while we're here," he said. "Have fun."

"Thanks," I said, tucking the phone into my pocket. Mom was going to find a ton of crazy-fun-house-mirror selfies on this thing tomorrow!

I was headed toward the International Pavilion when the phone rang. It was Cat.

"Hi, Cat," I answered.

"Maggie?" Cat sounded confused.

"No. It's Blaire. I have Mom's phone."

"Oh, good. I was calling for you anyway. I'm at the vintage dress store with my bridesmaids."

My heart skipped a beat as I remembered how our trip to Kellenberger's had ended. But if Cat was shopping for dresses, she hadn't called off the wedding. That was good.

"I've found two awesome gowns," Cat was saying. "Shannon likes one, but Maya likes the other. I love them both and can't decide. Will you be the tiebreaker?"

"Of course!" I said. "I'm at the fair, so send me pictures on Mom's phone."

It was almost one o'clock, so I picked up my pace, staring at the phone as I went. I walked straight into a little girl holding a giant stuffed banana. "Oops, sorry!" I told her.

I found a seat at the pavilion with two minutes to spare. *Come on, Cat! Show me those dresses!* What was taking her so long? I shook the phone in frustration.

"Cell phone service is terrible around here," said a woman sitting next to me.

Ding! Finally, the first photo popped up. Wow, that dress was beautiful. And Cat was glowing! I waited for the second photo to come through.

"Come on, come on," I whispered. There was movement near the stage as members of the dance troupe entered the pavilion.

Come on, Cat . . .

The dancers were now onstage and had formed a semicircle. The leader of Thea's troupe stepped up to the microphone to welcome the audience.

Ding! The second photo came in. That dress was gorgeous, too! But my gut said the first one was the winner. I quickly typed a reply and pressed SEND as the first notes of the music started. I tucked the phone into my pocket and looked up to see Thea and Madison onstage.

Wait, what? What happened to the other dancers?

Oh! The duet! It was weeks ago that Thea talked about trying out for it. And she got it!

"Woo-hoo!" I sat up straighter and cheered for my friend.

Thea and Madison were amazing. I could tell by the way the other dancers watched them in awe that this duet *was* a big deal, just like Thea had said at her rehearsal that day. That was my friend up there, and she was rocking it!

But as the dance went on, my excitement slowly turned into a lump in my throat.

Why hadn't Thea told me she got the duet? That was exactly the kind of Big News you're supposed to share with your BFF. Like when I had Big News about Gabe proposing or Cat agreeing to let me help with the wedding, Thea was the first person I called.

As Thea and Madison pulled off some complicated footwork, I flashed back to the day Thea went to the swimming hole with Madison. She hadn't told me about that either. What else hadn't she shared?

After the performance, Thea and I found each other in a crowd of her dance friends and their families. We hugged, but it was awkward. I drew away quicker than usual.

"You were great," I said. "I loved those turns at the end of the duet."

"Thanks," she said stiffly. "It means a lot to me that you were here. I was afraid you'd have to cancel again because of wedding stuff."

I shook my head. "I wouldn't miss this! I know how important it is to you."

Thea's expression softened, and I let out a breath I didn't know I was holding. "So," she said, linking her arm through mine. "Should we get something to eat?"

"Definitely," I said. "There's a funnel cake calling our names." I steered us through the crowd in the direction of the funnel cake booth.

"Hey, wait," Thea said, stopping short. "I was thinking maybe we could share a jumbo cotton candy this year. Since we can't get the whipped cream on the funnel cake, maybe we could start a new tradition. One that doesn't mess with your lactose issues."

"We always get funnel cake," I said.

"But the whipped cream—"

"Thea," I said, more loudly than I meant to. "I KNOW what I can't have. Why do you always have to remind me?!"

Thea's eyes widened. She looked hurt. "Well, sorry for caring."

"Forget the food," I said, shaking my head. "Let's just do the fun house before it gets too crowded."

We headed down the midway in silence. Everyone around us looked like they were having a blast—the kind of awesome time Thea and I were supposed to be having.

We showed the attendant our wristbands and stepped inside the fun house to my favorite part—the mirror maze. Thea ran ahead, and suddenly there were a million Theas in front of me. I felt a twinge in my stomach. It was like all those girls weren't just Thea but also our other friends and her dance buddies, whom she'd been hanging out with all summer instead of me.

"Come on," said Thea and her infinite clones, waving me deeper into the maze. She stopped in front of a mirror that made her look super short, as if she'd been smushed into a mini version of herself. I stepped up to the mirror next to it, which made me look freaky-tall. Mom's phone stuck out of my front pocket. It looked bigger than my head!

"Whoa, can you imagine if phones were really that giant?" I said, letting out a laugh.

"Yeah," Thea said, examining my reflection. "You probably wouldn't carry them around everywhere if they were that big. And I guess you'd be forced to actually watch a dance performance instead of texting."

I pivoted to face Thea. "What's that supposed to mean?"

Thea looked angry. "I barely see you all summer, and then when I do . . . you're on your phone instead of watching my performance."

Huh? "I did watch your performance! I just had to deal with a wedding situation first. Cat was—"

"Enough about the wedding," Thea said. "I don't want to hear any more wedding talk."

"What happened to you being excited about the wedding and helping?" I asked her, but she had already raced up the stairs to the second level of the fun house where there's a bunch of moving platforms you can walk across. I followed her.

Thea was on a platform that went up and down when I got upstairs. I jumped on one that wobbled back and forth. We were going in totally different directions.

"What happened to you being excited about the wedding and helping me out?" I repeated.

"I didn't know you'd get totally obsessed and not want to do anything else," Thea said. "Or talk about anything else—like the things I'm doing."

"But you didn't even tell me you got the duet!" I said.

"I tried to tell you on the phone yesterday," Thea said. "But you didn't have time to talk—because of course you were too busy with wedding stuff."

"This wedding's important to me!" I yelled, losing my balance and grabbing the railing next to the platform. "I want Cat to be happy. I want Grandpa to stay. If you were a good friend, you'd get that."

"And if *you* were a good friend, you wouldn't have totally abandoned me this summer."

I jumped off the platform. My head was spinning. "I abandoned *you?* No! You abandoned me, even though you promised to help."

Thea stepped off her own platform. "Forget this fair thing, okay? I'm done." She turned and ran at top speed, out of the fun house, away from me.

CHAPTER 18

Pressure

As soon as Dad's truck pulled up to the house, I scrambled out of it and headed straight inside.

Grandpa was at the front desk. "How was the fair?" he called.

"Fine," I mumbled, rushing past him to the stairs. I was on the second-floor landing when I heard Dad come in.

"What's up with Blaire?" Grandpa asked Dad.

"I'm not sure," Dad answered. "She said Thea got a ride home from someone else but she didn't say another word on the way home."

When I got to my room, I slammed the door, which made something fall off my inspiration board. It was the photo strip of me and Thea from last year's fair. I kicked it under my bed, then curled up in a ball on top of my covers.

There was a knock at my door, and Mom poked her head in. "Are you okay, sweetie? Did something happen with Thea today?"

The drama in the fun house played on a loop in my head. I felt angry and sad and confused. How could I explain any of it to Mom? Finally, I just said, "We had a fight."

Mom sat down on the edge of my bed. "Do you want to talk?"

I shook my head. "I just want to be by myself for a while."

"Okay," Mom said, tucking a strand of hair behind my ear. "But you know where I am if you need me."

After Mom left, I reached for my tablet. I needed a distraction from the day. Maybe there was something new posted on my favorite animal channel.

But not even a video called "Goats Wearing Pajamas" could cheer me up.

꙰

I tossed and turned all night, then slept later than usual. It was midmorning before I finally got up and went outside. I wandered to the gazebo and was surprised to find

Cat there, drinking a cup of coffee while gazing at the creek.

"Hey, Sprout," she said when she saw me. "Thanks for breaking that wedding gown tie yesterday. You were right. The first dress was The One. I bought it!"

I sat down next to her. "That's great." But I realized that if I hadn't been looking at the photos Cat sent me, Thea and I wouldn't have had our fight.

"I'm sorry. Are you Blaire *Wilson*?" Cat asked, peering into my eyes "The Blaire I know would be jumping up and down at the news that I bought a wedding dress."

"Sorry," I said. "I didn't sleep well last night. Thea and I had a fight yesterday."

Cat put her coffee cup down. "Oh no. Do you want to tell me about it?"

I shrugged. I did *not* want to tell Cat that it had anything to do with her wedding. "I'm still trying to figure it out."

"I get that," Cat said. "Gabe and I had a bit of a disagreement yesterday, too."

"Wedding stuff?" I asked.

Cat nodded. "What else? Planning something this big, this fast has put a lot of pressure on us." Cat placed her arm around my shoulder. "On all of us."

I felt tears stinging my eyes. Maybe I *could* tell Cat about my fight with Thea. But before I could say anything, Gabe appeared.

"There you are!" he said to Cat. "I have good news! Blaire—you'll love this too. My mother called *Empire State Weddings* magazine and told them about the new Pleasant View Farm barn venue. And guess what? They want to write a review!"

Empire State Weddings? I flashed back to that day at Kellenberger's when I'd shown the magazine to Cat with Mrs. V right there. I never imagined Mrs. V would actually contact them!

"Oh my gosh," I said, suddenly feeling excited. "Mrs. V had an idea-spark!"

But Cat looked doubtful. "Really?" she asked. "Is that okay with Daniel and Maggie? It's their barn."

Gabe nodded. "I just told Daniel." Gabe looked at me. "Your dad thinks it's going to be great for the farm."

"What will they review, exactly?" Cat asked.

"The barn, of course. But they want to see an actual wedding here, so they're going to attend ours."

"Wow!" I said. "That's so cool. Your wedding will be in a magazine, Cat!"

"Wait a minute," Cat said. "I don't want my wedding in a magazine, and I don't want some stranger taking notes on my wedding and—and—*judging* it for their magazine readers. Gabe, I don't think this is a good idea."

"You don't?" Gabe looked completely surprised. "I thought you'd be excited. I—I already said yes."

"You WHAT?" Cat exploded.

Gabe's eyes widened. "Well, it would be great publicity for the farm, so Mom and I assumed you'd want to—"

"You and *your mom* made this decision?" Cat said. "Why didn't you and *I* make this decision, Gabe?"

Gabe and I looked at each other, too stunned to speak.

"This is too much," Cat finally said to Gabe. She shook her head. "You and I are taking a break. And this wedding?" Her voice broke. "This wedding is off!"

CHAPTER 19

Apologies

Pleasant View Farm is like Earth: it keeps spinning no matter what happens, even on afternoons when weddings of my almost-big-sister get canceled. Mom and the kitchen staff were cooking. Dad was working on the barn. And I was cleaning out the chicken coop while the chickens grazed in the field.

I was scooping straw out of the nesting boxes when Grandpa appeared. "Blaire!" he said, sounding concerned. "I just heard about Cat calling off the wedding. I'm sorry, sweetheart."

I dumped the old straw on the ground. "At least it means *you'll* stay."

"Stay where?" Grandpa asked.

"Here," I said. "At the farm."

Grandpa's brows knit together in confusion. "Huh?"

"We can't ruin Pleasant View Farm if the wedding never happens." I sighed.

"Blaire Wilson, I'm still not following."

I stopped scooping and turned to Grandpa. "You said weddings at the barn would ruin everything we spent so many years building. You said maybe it was time for you to retire. You said maybe you'd . . . move out if the first barn event was a failure." My throat felt tight.

"When did I say these things?" Grandpa asked.

"At Freddy's, the day we got Penny and Dash," I said, picking up a clean mound of straw. "I heard you and Freddy talking in his living room."

Grandpa thought for a moment, then shook his head. "Oh, sweetheart! I didn't mean I'd *actually* move out! I was grumpy and sad because my friend was losing his farm."

My heart skipped a beat. "So you won't leave?" I asked. "No matter what happens with the barn?"

"Blaire, I would never leave you or my family or our farm. This place, and the people here, are my life."

I was so relieved that I dropped my pile of straw and threw my arms around Grandpa. "You sounded so serious that day at Freddy's. I believed you!"

Grandpa wrapped his arms around me and laughed. "Well, you can't believe everything you hear. Look, my job is to make sure we never lose sight of what this farm is about. I don't like the idea of this new party barn, but I believe in our family, and I'll always stick with you."

I was afraid I would cry if I said anything else, so I just gave Grandpa another ginormous hug.

"Now," Grandpa said, pulling away to look at my face. "What's going on with you? You were in quite the mood when you got home from the fair yesterday."

I told Grandpa all about my fight with Thea. "She said I abandoned her this summer," I said, picking up clean straw and filling a nesting box.

Grandpa scooped up an armload of straw and filled another box. "Well, Thea's right," he said.

"What?" I squealed.

"You've gotten so wrapped up in barn renovations and wedding plans that you've stopped doing a whole bunch of stuff," Grandpa said, reaching for more straw. "It's good to have a passion that fires you up. But you have to find a balance. You need time to have fun, and time with your family and friends, too."

I started raking up the straw on the ground, thinking about how many times I'd changed or canceled plans with Thea or said *no* to invitations from her or our other friends. I shrugged. "Hanging out at the farm is just easier. Every time I go somewhere with my friends, there's something I can't eat. It makes me feel like I'm a blob of lactose intolerance instead of a person."

"Ah, I see." Grandpa rested an elbow on the top of the nesting box. "I can only imagine how hard it is for you to adjust to your diagnosis, but retreating from your friends—or getting lost in that tablet of yours—won't make your food issue go away."

I raked in silence until Grandpa said, "I believe you owe Thea an apology."

"Maybe I do." I sighed. "But she owes me one, too. She promised she'd help with the wedding planning and she didn't. It's not okay."

"Then talk to her. I'm sure she has a good reason for that, just like you thought you had a good reason for putting all your time and energy into the wedding."

I rolled my eyes. "Okay. I'll text her and—"

"Not on that dang screen of yours," Grandpa corrected me. "The real way. *In person*."

꘏꘏꘏

"Blaire!" Mrs. Dimitriou exclaimed. I was standing on their front porch "I haven't seen you since Thea's party. Come on in!"

"What are you doing here?" asked Thea from the top of the stairs inside.

"I brought you a peace offering." I held out a pinwheel I'd made. I had tied a bow out of some leftover fabric from Thea's birthday gift around the stick. "I was hoping we could talk."

Thea came slowly downstairs and took the pinwheel. "Thanks," she said, blowing on it to make it twirl. "Let's go out back."

Thea's yard was small, but it had a patio and a play set with two swings. When we were younger, we used to play there for hours at a time.

After Thea stuck the pinwheel into the soil of a flower box, we both stood back to admire it. Then Thea took the swing she liked best. I sat down on the other.

"I'm sorry," I said.

Thea raised an eyebrow.

"I know I've been obsessed with the wedding," I continued. "But I didn't mean to abandon you. Here's the thing." I explained how rough it had been getting used to my new normal. "Keeping busy at the farm was my way to just not deal with the fact that every time I went out, I was faced with stuff I couldn't eat, and embarrassing conversations about it."

We swung back and forth for a few moments, the creaking of the chains filling the silence.

"I didn't think of that," Thea finally said. "You just know so much about food that I figured it wasn't a big deal."

After another few moments of silent swinging, I took a deep breath and said, "Why did you stop helping with the wedding?"

"I'm sorry," Thea said quickly. "I know I promised I would, and I bailed. I wanted to spend time with you, but Blaire, barn renovation really isn't my thing, *dahling.*"

I nodded.

Thea jumped off her swing and stood facing me. "I started hanging out with Madison because it felt better to spend time with friends who *were* around. But I missed you so much!"

I stopped swinging. "You did?"

Thea nodded.

"I missed you, too," I said.

Thea sat back down on her swing. "Sorry if you thought I didn't miss you. I guess there's only so much you can say with texting, even if you add emojis and GIFs."

"It's okay," I said. Then I had an idea-spark. "Wait, what if we had a special secret emoji between us that we could use when we're not sure what a text or email means? Like, a way to say, *I don't understand. Let's talk in person.*"

Thea grinned. "Ha, I love it! How about . . ." Thea and I both thought for a few moments.

"The speak-no-evil monkey!" we called out at the same time, slapping our hands over our mouths. Twin idea-sparks!

"Perfect," I said. "I think Cat and Gabe need a signal, too."

"What?" Thea asked. "Why?"

"Cat called the wedding off."

Thea gasped. "No! Seriously? But why?"

We climbed up to the little fort at the top of the play set, and I told her about Mrs. V inviting *Empire State Weddings* and how that was the last straw for Cat. "It's sort of my fault." I sighed. "Mrs. V and I kinda got carried away."

"Hmmm," said Thea. "Do you think Cat still wants to marry Gabe?"

I shrugged. "I don't know. She won't talk to me about Gabe or the wedding."

"Do you think they still love each other?"

"I do. But right now they're not talking to each other."

Thea shook her head. "We have to change that."

Idea-spark! "Come inside," I said to Thea, borrowing her evil villain voice. "I have a brilliant plan."

CHAPTER 20

Wherefore Art Thou, Cat?

"I got your text," Cat said breathlessly as she jogged up to the orchard. "What's wrong?"

"We have a problem," I said.

"We wrote this play as an extra credit summer project for school," Thea explained, waving a stack of papers. "But we need two more people to practice it with us."

Cat put her hands on her hips. "A PLAY? You said this was an emergency!"

"It is!" I said.

We heard the squeaking of bike pedals and turned to see Gabe riding toward us. When he spotted Cat, he screeched to a stop and hopped off.

"Uh, where's the emergency?" he asked, confused. "Cat, are you okay?"

Cat nodded without looking at him. "There's no emergency," she said, sounding annoyed. "Just a play these two want us to help with."

Gabe looked confused.

"Cat, please!" I said. "We worked hard on this play. We need your help!"

Cat sighed. "I'll give it five minutes." She glanced at Gabe and he gave her a little smile.

Aha, I thought. *At least they'll still look at each other.*

Thea passed out the scripts. "I'll be Mia," she said, "and Blaire will be Claire, and—"

"Let me guess," Gabe said, skimming the script. "Cat will be Nat, and I'll be . . . *Schmabe?*"

"Yup!" I said. "Okay, I have the first line. 'Woe is me, dear Mia! The Lady Nat called off her wedding with Sir Schmabe.'"

Thea started reading: "'Oh, Lady Claire, what could possibly come between two people who are so happily in love?'"

"'Perhaps an evil curse,'" I said as Lady Claire. "'But wait—here is Sir Schmabe now, riding his pegasus.'"

I glanced at Cat out of the corner of my eye. Her face was flushed. Was she angry?

"Gabe, it's your line," said Thea.

Gabe cleared his throat and began to read. "'Nat! Dear Nat! Wherefore art thou? We have not spoken in so long!'"

I nudged Cat, because that was her cue. "'I'm here, Sir Schmabe,'" she read in a flat voice. "'I have been busy fixing my spacecraft so I can return to Earth . . .'" Cat looked up from her script. "Wait a sec. Where exactly does this take place?"

"Not sure," Thea said. "It's a work in progress. Gabe. Line."

"'Before you leave this planet,'" Gabe read, "'would you join me for a farewell picnic lunch in the golden gazebo? I went to the deli on Planet Bluefield and got your favorite—'" Gabe's voice caught. "'Your favorite,'" he continued after he cleared his throat. "'The Intergalactic Turkey Sub.'"

"'That does sound out-of-this-world delicious,'" Cat said as Nat. She looked over at me with an expression that said *I know what you're up to.*

"'And perhaps after that,'" Gabe continued, "'we could take a stroll around the Orbital Orchards, ours hands intertwined— '" Gabe raised an eyebrow at Thea and me, then took a step toward Cat. "Um . . . it says here I'm supposed to take your hand. May I?"

Cat hesitated. Thea and I looked at each other, holding our breath.

Finally, Cat nodded.

"'Our hands intertwined like the branches of the trees above,'" Gabe finished.

It was Cat's line, but she just stood there, staring down at her hand in Gabe's. "I think it's your line, Nat," Gabe whispered to her.

Cat swallowed hard, then turned back to her script. "'Oh, Schmabe! That would make me happier than . . .'" She dropped the script to her waist and looked up at Gabe. "Well, happier than I've been in a while."

I glanced at Thea. This wasn't in the script, but I liked where it was going!

Gabe put his script down. "I've missed you."

"I've missed you, too," Cat said. "I've done a lot of thinking these last few days. I know for sure that I don't want some over-the-top wedding. But I know something else for sure, too. Sir Schmabe," she said, her voice strong, "would you do me the honor of —"

"Wait thee a second, Nat," Gabe said, improvising now. "Are you asking me if I want to marry you?"

Cat nodded.

"I do," Gabe said, folding her in his arms. Then he pulled away quickly. "Oh, wait, I should save that for the wedding!" They both smiled. Then they hugged again, for real.

Thea and I high-fived each other.

"I like how this play ended," Gabe said to me and Thea over Cat's head, which was still resting on his shoulder.

"You get an A-plus on your summer extra credit project," added Cat, her voice muffled by Gabe's shirt.

"Blaire? Is that you?" Mrs. V's face popped up on my tablet screen. She was wearing a towel wrapped around her hair and her skin was . . . green. "I'm doing a mint cucumber mask! I've been so upset since Cat called off the wedding, I've had to give myself a calming facial *every* night!"

"Well then, I have some awesome news for you," I said. "The wedding is back on."

"WHAT?" Mrs. V sat up so quickly that the towel almost fell off her head. "Oh my! That's marvelous! But now we have so much to do!"

"Actually . . ." I began, "Cat has changed the decor a bit. She and I will handle it all from here."

Mrs. V frowned. "Changed? Still 'farm fancy,' I hope?"

"Of course. It's going to be perfect. And with you there, Mrs. V, the 'fancy' part is totally covered."

Mrs. V broke into a big smile. Then her towel slid onto the phone and the screen went dark.

CHAPTER 21

Racing Against the Clock

I t was all hands on deck. Or actually, all hands on *barn*.

The wedding was in five days and we were racing against the clock. Dad had hired a crew to paint the outside of the barn, but we still had to paint the window trim and do some other finishing touches before we could decorate.

Thea and I painted the trim with small brushes, making it fun by playing a real-life game of This or That. I set my watch so that every hour we would take a break to go see Dash and Penny.

Halfway through the first workday, Grandpa came in and offered to help.

"The finish on this part of the floor looks a little uneven," he said to Dad. "Mind if I do some sanding?"

"Do I *mind*?" asked Dad. "That would be fantastic, Ben. Please, do whatever you think needs to be done."

The next morning, Dad recruited Beckett to help with the painting. We'd been working for about an hour when there was a knock on the open doorway.

"Helloooooo!" called a familiar voice.

Mrs. V waved from the barn entrance. She was dressed in a long-sleeved white jumpsuit with a rhinestone-studded belt, and a white leather cap.

"Mom?" Gabe said. "What are you doing here?"

"I heard you were painting, so I'm here to help. Look, I found the perfect outfit for it."

She spun around. The jumpsuit had a paintbrush made out of rhinestones on the back! We all laughed.

"I have just the job for you," Dad said.

He teamed her up with Beckett to finish painting the window trim. Beckett grinned, and Mrs. V said, "Would you empty your pockets before we begin working together? I want to make sure you're not going to spring another dead frog on me."

Finally, with two days to go, the painting and other final touches were done. We'd set up tables and chairs, and tomorrow we would decorate.

I found Mom in the restaurant kitchen and gave her an update. While most of us had been working on the event space, Mom had been working on the food.

"What are you making?" I asked.

"I'm doing some prep for the appetizers for the wedding," she said. She let out a big yawn.

"Do you need help?"

"I sure do, but there are some dairy ingredients in these. I know it makes you uncomfortable to cook with what you can't eat."

"It did," I said, nodding. But I realized that that was at the beginning of the summer, when I was first getting used to my diagnosis. I still didn't like being dairy-free, but I *did* like not feeling sick all the time. This new normal was starting to feel . . . kind of normal. "I think I should try again," I told Mom.

"Oh, Blaire, that's great!" Mom pulled me in for a hug.

Mom always says that cooking is a form of love. There was no way I was going to let my food issues stop me from showing Cat and Gabe how much I love them.

CHAPTER 22

Sharing This Moment

I stood at the edge of the orchard, holding my bouquet of wildflowers. I was surprised that my hands were shaking.

"You okay?" Thea whispered, straightening the sash at my back. I felt like the fanciest junior bridesmaid in my blue dress with its delicate floral pattern. The cap sleeves were so sheer, they felt like fairy wings. My favorite part was the skirt, which was longer in the back than the front. I basically never wanted to take it off.

"I'm nervous," I whispered back. "And excited. *Nervous-ited.*"

"That makes two of us," Cat said from behind the row of bridesmaids.

"There's no need to be nervous," Thea assured us. "At this point, what could possibly go wrong?"

Thea took her seat as the guitar player started "Here Comes the Sun." That was my cue. Gabe, standing in front of the gazebo, gave me a small nod. He looked completely relaxed.

I took a deep breath. Here we go. One foot in front of the other.

As I started walking down the aisle, everyone turned to look. All those smiles felt like spotlights shining on me. I thought about what Grandpa had told me this morning. "Just enjoy the moment."

So instead of focusing on my nerves, I focused on how beautiful everything was. We had decorated the gazebo with wildflowers from the field and copper-colored paper fans that shimmered in the sun. I saw the arch to the orchard, which was draped in lavender tulle. The nearby apple trees were hung with more coppery paper fans, which swayed gently in the breeze. It was all simple and romantic and perfect.

I made it to the gazebo and took my place on one side. Dad, Mom, and Grandpa beamed at me from their seats in the front row. Beckett rolled his eyes and tugged at the bow tie around his neck.

After Gabe's two groomsmen walked Cat's brides-maids down the aisle, everyone rose. Cat practically floated across the lawn. She was wearing a sleeveless cream-colored dress overlaid with lace. Her brother, in his military dress uniform, looked so proud to be escorting Cat down the aisle.

When they reached the gazebo, Lorenzo kissed Cat on the cheek. She squeezed his hand, and I could see both of them tearing up. I knew without a doubt it had been worth it, to rush the planning so that he could be here.

Lorenzo took his place next to Mom, and everyone sat down. Cat took a deep breath and stepped toward Gabe. She looked more nervous than I'd ever seen her.

But instead of taking Cat's hand to lead her into the gazebo, where the minister was waiting, Gabe turned, picked up a bag from the ground, and pulled out a sandwich.

HUH?!

"Turkey sub?" he asked.

Cat started laughing.

"What, we're not just having a picnic in the gazebo?" Gabe asked with a straight face. Then he grinned and tossed the sandwich to one of this groomsmen, who unwrapped one end and took a big bite. All of the guests cracked up.

As Gabe took Cat's hand and led her to the gazebo, I could see that Cat wasn't nervous anymore. Gabe's sandwich stunt had calmed her down. *That's why they were meant to be together.*

⚜

After the ceremony, as Cat and Gabe posed for pictures in the gazebo, Dad introduced me to the reporter from *Empire State Weddings*. Cat had agreed to let someone from the magazine review the wedding because she knew the exposure would be good for the farm. It was her gift to us for hosting her wedding.

"Blaire helped plan the wedding," Dad told the reporter. "She did all the decorations herself."

The woman from the magazine nodded and wrote something in her notebook.

"Wait till you see the barn," I told her, hoping she would be impressed with it.

Cat and Gabe climbed onto the tandem bike, which Thea and I had decorated with wildflowers and lavender colored ribbons. As they set off through the orchard, the guitarist played "A Bicycle Built for Two." Cat and Gabe rode under the arch and down the path to the barn, which was lined with luminarias we'd light later in the evening. The wedding guests followed on foot, and Thea and I hurried ahead to make sure everything was ready.

Once we were inside the barn, Thea flipped the switch on Mrs. V's bubble machine. As my eyes adjusted from the bright sunshine, I saw bubbles floating out into the breeze, and vases of wildflowers wrapped in tulle, and chickens pecking the floorboards near the head table.

Wait. *Chickens?!*

They were everywhere. Chickens strutted across the dance floor and hopped up onto the bales of hay that had been set up to hold gifts. Several were perched on the newly painted windowsills. Dandelion was next to the chicken crate card box, examining the painted eggs.

"Dandy, no," I said, scooping up the Silkie.

Behind me, Thea said, "Um, I don't remember this as part of the plan."

"Thea, we have to get the chickens out of here before anyone else sees. Quick—close the front door!"

"Too late," Thea whispered, as Cat and Gabe appeared. Mrs. V was right behind them, with the magazine reporter beside her.

"You're going to love this space," Mrs. V was saying to the reporter. "It's absolutely perfect—"

"Better make that *bird*fect," Thea said as Mrs. V let out a shriek. The reporter started scribbling something in her notebook.

I looked at Cat, horrified that her reception was overrun with chickens. But Cat just started laughing. As guests began streaming in, she greeted them by saying, "Welcome to farm fancy!"

"Yes," Gabe added. "Find your seat. It may include a free chicken."

"Well, at least Cat and Gabe don't seem too upset," Thea said to me.

"Thank goodness for that," I agreed, handing Dandy to Thea. "But we're going to have to explain this to the magazine reporter." I saw Beckett come into the barn, and I waved him over.

Beckett looked guilty as he crossed the room. "I guess I must have left the coop open after I collected the eggs this morning," he said. "I'm really sorry."

"We'll talk later," I said, pointing to his bow tie. "Right now, I need that."

"Take it!" he said, pulling off the tie. "It's choking me."

"Thanks. Now get me one other chicken, and then get the rest of them out of here."

I tore a piece of tulle fabric off one of the center-pieces, pulled a flower from my bouquet, and made a mini makeshift veil. I managed to tuck the veil into the feathers on Dandy's head.

Beckett handed me another chicken. I took the bow tie and slipped it over the bird's head.

Ta-da! Picture-perfect junior bride and groom. We presented the chickens to Cat and Gabe, who laughed as they posed for photos with them.

The magazine reporter took some photos and then came over to me. "This is quite the setup," she said. To my amazement and relief, she sounded impressed.

"Oh, you know," I said. "We do whatever we can to make weddings special here at Pleasant View Farm."

⚜

Once Beckett and Thea got all of the chickens out of barn and we did some fast cleanup, the waitstaff came through with trays of appetizers. I watched one guest try the spinach cheese puffs I'd helped Mom make. She smiled after she took a bite, then reached for another one. I couldn't have any, but it sure made me happy to know she was enjoying them.

When it was time for dinner, Grandpa held out my chair so I could sit down. Then he took the chair next to mine. "Well, Blaire," he said, "I think you pulled it off. Are you happy?"

"I am," I said, nodding. "Are *you* happy?"

"I am," he admitted. He paused and looked around the room. "You know, I wish my parents could see this happening in their old, run-down barn."

"I think they'd be pleased that we created this place for people to come together, don't you?"

Grandpa put his arm around me. "I think you're right. I never thought I'd hear myself say this, but bring on more weddings!"

When dinner was finished, Cat and Gabe fed each other spoonfuls of crème brûlée. Mom brought me a dish of the dairy-free version and I dug right in. Even if I find out that I can start eating dairy again, this coconut crème brûlée will be a keeper.

I was scraping up the last delicious bite when Cat and Gabe took the microphone from the DJ. "We want to thank everyone for celebrating with us," Gabe said. "And we want to thank the Wilsons for making this such an incredible day."

"We owe a special thanks to Blaire Wilson," Cat added. "Sprout, this song is for you."

With that, the DJ started playing "Do the Funky Chicken." Mrs. Vandegriff and Lorenzo were the first on the dance floor, followed by Gabe and Cat, then Mom and Dad. Thea grabbed Beckett and they began strutting around the dance floor, pretending to be chickens.

I went to get Mom's phone to take some pictures. But then I saw the wedding photographer shooting candids of all the dancers, and I realized there would be plenty of photos. So I headed to the dance floor, too. The best way to enjoy this moment was sharing it with the people I loved, right here, right now.

I stepped on the dance floor and flapped my arms like chicken wings.

Everything's good.

ABOUT THE AUTHOR

Jennifer Castle grew up writing stories in her head on long school bus rides and was constantly looking for ways to turn her idea-sparks into reality. These included dozens of poems, a homemade magazine that lasted three issues, a barrette-making business, and a cruise boat made of branches and cardboard for the creek behind her house. Eventually, one of her "big ideas" became a published novel, and since then she has written more than ten books for kids and teens, including the Butterfly Wishes series, *Together at Midnight*, and *Famous Friends*. Jennifer lives among the mountains, woods, and bountiful farms of New York's Hudson Valley with her husband, two daughters, and two striped cats, who also work part-time as her writing assistants.

SPECIAL THANKS

With gratitude to Lindsey Lusher Shute, Executive Director and Co-founder of the National Young Farmers Coalition and co-owner of Hearty Roots Community Farm in New York's Hudson Valley; Dr. Amanda Cox, Assistant Professor of Pediatrics in the Division of Pediatric Allergy and Immunology and fellow of the American Academy of Allergy, Asthma, and Immunology; Dr. Megan Moreno, Academic Division Chief: General Pediatrics and Adolescent Medicine, Vice Chair of Digital Health, and Principal Investigator of the Social Media and Adolescent Health Research Team (SMAHRT); and Kamille Adamany, Director of Restaurants at American Girl, for their insights and knowledge.

Ready to
COOK UP more
FUN with
Blaire?

VISIT

americangirl.com to learn more about Blaire's world!

Parents, request a FREE catalogue at
americangirl.com/catalogue

Sign up at **americangirl.com/email**
to receive the latest news and exclusive offers

★ American Girl®

A group of girls so close, they're just

Like Sisters

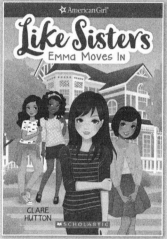

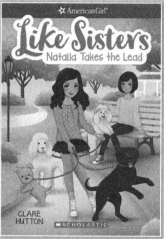

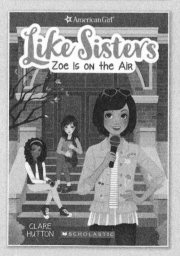